A TRAP

Rich took the stairs two at a time. The door to their room was standing open, and he sighed with relief. He went straight in, not thinking it might be a trap.

As soon as he was through the door, everything went black. He had time to cry out in surprise and alarm—just once. Then he was fighting against the blanket that was tight over his face and shoulders. Rich was being dragged out of the room and back down the stairs. His feet caught on the threadbare carpet and knocked painfully against the wall of the stairwell as he was bundled away.

Soon he was on level ground again, the thin lounge carpet under his feet. Then he heard his feet scrape on the bare stone floor of the lobby, followed by the warm breeze on his hands and a brightness even through the blanket. He was struggling to speak, but his throat was clogged with dust and whenever he tried, he ended up coughing and choking. There were uneven cobbles under his feet now. His head was pushed roughly down and he was shoved forward—landing on something soft. A chair? Where was he?

An engine revved. A door slammed. Rich was in a car, and it was pulling away.

OTHER BOOKS YOU MAY ENJOY

JACK HIGGINS

WITH JUSTIN RICHARDS

DEATH RUN

speak

An Imprint of Penguin Group (USA) Inc.

SPEAK

Published by the Penguin Group

Penguin Group (USA) Inc., 345 Hudson Street, New York, New York 10014, U.S.A.

Penguin Group (Canada), 90 Eglinton Avenue East, Suite 700, Toronto, Ontario, Canada M4P 2Y3
(a division of Pearson Penguin Canada Inc.)

Penguin Books Ltd, 80 Strand, London WC2R 0RL, England

Penguin Ireland, 25 St Stephen's Green, Dublin 2, Ireland (a division of Penguin Books Ltd)

Penguin Group (Australia), 250 Camberwell Road, Camberwell, Victoria 3124, Australia
(a division of Pearson Australia Group Pty Ltd)

Penguin Books India Pvt Ltd, 11 Community Centre, Panchsheel Park, New Delhi - 110 017, India

Penguin Group (NZ), 67 Apollo Drive, Rosedale, North Shore 0632, New Zealand
(a division of Pearson New Zealand Ltd)

Penguin Books (South Africa) (Pty) Ltd, 24 Sturdee Avenue,
Rosebank, Johannesburg 2196, South Africa

Registered Offices: Penguin Books Ltd, 80 Strand, London WC2R 0RL, England

First published in Great Britain by HarperCollins Children's Books, 2007
First American edition published by G. P. Putnam's Sons,
a division of Penguin Young Readers Group, 2008
Published by Speak, an imprint of Penguin Group (USA) Inc., 2009

1 3 5 7 9 10 8 6 4 2

THE LIBRARY OF CONGRESS HAS CATALOGED THE G. P. PUTNAM'S SONS EDITION AS FOLLOWS:

Higgins, Jack, date.
Death run / by Jack Higgins with Justin Richards.—1st American ed.   p. cm.
Summary: A mafia banker with access to a large number of criminal accounts is willing to
give evidence in exchange for help retiring from the mob, but when spy John Chance assists
him, he puts his fifteen-year-old twins, Rich and Jade, in the line of fire.
ISBN: 978-0-399-25081-1 (hc)
[1. Spies—Fiction. 2. Organized crime—Fiction. 3. Fathers—Fiction. 4. Twins—Fiction.
5. Brothers and sisters—Fiction. 6. Adventure and adventurers—Fiction.
7. Venice (Italy)—Fiction. 8. Italy—Fiction. 9. England—Fiction.] I. Richards, Justin.
II. Title.
PZ7.H534954Dea 2008 [Fic]—dc22 2007042830

Speak ISBN 978-0-14-241475-0

Printed in the United States of America

Design by Katrina Damkoehler
Text set in Plantin

DEATH RUN

PROLOGUE

They arrived in Mont Passat just four hours before the alarms went off. Rich, Jade and their father had a suite of rooms above the main casino. They were spacious and plush, the whole place furnished like the nineteenth-century European palace it once was. Room service provided food that looked like it had been placed on the plate by an artist. Jade's mineral water and Dad's champagne were entirely in keeping, but Rich's Coke seemed out of place in its cut-glass tumbler.

It had only been a few months since Rich and Jade first met John Chance. Until then they hadn't even known they had a father. But after Mum was killed in a car accident, Dad had turned up at the funeral to look after them. The fifteen-year-old twins had resented him at first, but gradually, as they learned more about the man, they had come to respect and like—maybe even love—their dad. And beneath the gruff, hardened exterior Jade knew for sure he had come to respect and like—maybe even love—them.

"Can we play roulette and blackjack in the casino?" Rich asked as soon as he'd finished eating. "Will you teach us how to play poker?"

"No," said Dad.

"Gambling's addictive and you never win in the long run," Jade told her twin brother.

"Then what are we doing here?" Rich asked. He was slim and tall, like his sister. They both had blond hair and blue eyes, like their father. "I mean," Rich went on, "there's nothing in this place except the casino, is there? So, if we're going to Venice—why don't we just go to Venice?"

"Simple," Dad told them. Jade could tell from his tone he was making an effort to be patient. "I didn't book the tickets, all right? Ardman did."

"Might have known," Jade muttered. Ardman was Dad's boss. He ran some secret group that worked for the British prime minister's office and did "covert operations."

"So Ardman is sending us to Venice the long way," Rich said. "Why's that, then? Some secret job he wants you to do here in Mont Passat?"

"No," said Dad quickly. "I think Ardman's got some deal with the airline to get the cheapest tickets or take up spare capacity or something. His budget's under review by Sir Lionel Ffinch, the minister who is in charge of overseeing his department. We were lucky to get a holiday at all."

Dad suggested they make it an early night so they'd be refreshed for their early morning flight. Jade nodded in agreement, and Rich struggled to suppress his disappointment.

"Can't we at least check out the casino? Just look around? It's famous."

Dad shook his head. "You're too young. Have to be over twenty-one to get in." He grinned. "Tell you what—we can all come back in six years."

Jade and Rich headed for their bedrooms. Rich looked back at Dad. "I suppose you're going to be checking it out, though. Propping up the bar?"

"Absolutely not," Dad insisted. "I need my beauty sleep too, you know."

Jade laughed. "You're telling me."

Rich's bedroom was bigger than Dad's entire flat back in London. He didn't realize until he flopped down on the enormous bed how tired he was. It was an effort to get undressed, and before long, he was under the covers and drifting off to sleep.

The hand on his shoulder woke him immediately.

"Are you awake?" Jade was asking.

"I am now." Rich sat up. "What's up?"

His sister sat down on the bed beside him. She was in her pajamas and her hair was all over the place. "I couldn't sleep," she said.

Rich pulled his pillow over his head. "Your problem," he mumbled. "Deal with it."

"It's the noise."

"The casino?" Rich was obviously not going to be allowed to get to sleep either, so he emerged from the pillow. "I didn't notice it."

"Not the casino. Dad. His room's next to mine. You've got the living room or whatever it is between you."

"Dad? What's he doing?"

"Snoring." Jade got up from the bed. "Come and listen."

"Do I have to?"

"Yes."

"It can't be that bad," Rich protested. "We can swap rooms if you want."

They paused before they got halfway across the living room. The rhythmic sound of snoring echoed off the walls.

"Maybe not," Rich decided. "Still, at least we know he hasn't snuck off to the bar."

"I suppose." Jade slumped onto a small sofa. "It's good to know he hasn't just brought us here for the booze and the gambling."

In their father's room, the sound of loud snoring continued to emerge from the small digital recorder on the cabinet beside the empty bed. The windows out onto the balcony were open, and the curtains fluttered in the breeze.

• • •

The building was old and the stonework weathered enough to afford an easy grip. Chance had little difficulty climbing down from his room. He stood in the shadow of a large ornamental shrub to adjust his bow tie, straightened his dinner jacket and headed for the main entrance to the casino.

"Never again," he muttered under his breath as he smiled at the broad-shouldered doorman. "I'm on holiday." He silently cursed Ardman, made his way to the main bar and ordered a large whiskey.

This late in the evening, the casino was busy with the rich and the beautiful from all around the world. Old men with young women; mature women with young men. Chance was interested in none of them. He was intent on the men in suits who stood a little too stiffly, whose jackets bulged a little too much, who watched but never played or drank. It took him ten minutes before he was sure he had registered all the security staff.

What he did not see was the woman studying him from the shadows on the other side of the bar. Tall and slim, she wore a pale blue evening gown with an expensive-looking diamond necklace and matching earrings. Her hair was a startling auburn, and her eyes were bright blue.

Chance himself blended in well—an unremarkable man of about forty, with a rugged, experienced face. He could be a businessman enjoying an expensive night out, perhaps. No one special. No one memorable. It was an image that Chance cultivated. He liked not to be noticed. He finished his drink, left a tip that was just big enough to ensure the barman would not remember him and then went to the cloakroom.

"You're holding a briefcase for me," John Chance told the smartly dressed man at the desk. "The name is Enfield. Harrison Enfield."

"Of course, Mr. Enfield." The man's accent was French. He returned a moment later with a metal briefcase.

Chance opened the case and glanced inside—seeing exactly what he had expected. A wig, a false beard and an expensive suit in a small size. There was one other thing—a small metal box with a switch on the side. Chance took it out and slipped it into his pocket. He snapped the case closed and smiled his thanks to the young man.

From the raised area around the main roulette table, Chance had a good view of most of the casino floor. He placed a small bet on number seven and hoped he didn't win. Then, keeping his hand in his jacket pocket, he pressed the small button on the side of the metal box and started to count the seconds.

Chance knew that the moment he activated the device in his pocket, every one of the hidden surveillance cameras throughout the casino would go blind. The great thing about a wireless intranet system was that cameras could be put anywhere and they just radioed their pictures into the network. But if someone jammed the frequency, then everything would go black.

Twenty-one seconds after the cameras went blind, Chance saw the door to the main security control room open abruptly and a man come out. With fiery red hair and a beard to match, the man must have been fully six-and-a-half feet tall. He walked quickly and with an air of authority that did nothing to disguise his fury.

Pausing only to be sure the roulette wheel hadn't stopped at seven, Chance followed the red-haired man. He got as far as the first turn of the staircase leading up into the main hotel. Here there was a door marked STAFF ONLY. The man keyed a code into a pad beside the door and pushed through. Chance counted to four before he heard the sound of another door banging shut.

Chance pressed the button on the device again, turning it off. He had what he needed—for now. Ignoring the security-locked door, he continued up the steps to the next landing and waited. A few minutes later, the red-haired giant emerged again, this time with another man.

"The systems are back online now," the other man was saying. "I'm sure it's just a glitch. It can't be deliberate, Mr. Bannock."

Chance started down the stairs again, following just close enough to overhear.

"Let's not take the risk," the big man said. He had a thick Scottish accent, rolling the *r* of *risk* angrily. "If we lose the *property* now, there'll be hell to pay."

"He's quite safe where you put him," the smaller man said. "No pun intended."

Bannock grinned, his beard parting to reveal yellowed teeth.

Chance headed back to the roulette table and lost some more money. After twenty minutes, he pressed the button on the jamming device again and started to count. This time it was eight seconds. That was what Chance expected—they'd be quicker now, thinking it wasn't a onetime technical hitch. But if it continued . . .

The third time Chance only jammed the cameras for a few seconds before putting them back online. The control room door remained closed. The fourth time it was over a minute before Bannock emerged, and Chance immediately turned off the jammer again. He watched with satisfaction as a man in a dark suit chased after Bannock and was growled at for his trouble. *Yes,* Chance thought, *that should be enough.* Next time the security systems failed, they'd be sure it was a glitch, not deliberate sabotage. He made his way casually back to the main staircase.

Chance turned on the landing, heading past the staff-only door. As he turned, he once again activated the jammer and immediately returned to the number pad by the door. He'd seen Bannock—angry and therefore careless—key in a code. 5619. The door clicked open, and Chance was through.

He checked quickly for cameras and saw one covering the door. He moved out of its range and turned off the jammer. He planned to give them a minute to shout at each other, then he would kill the cameras again. In the meantime, he looked along the dimly lit corridor, working out which door Bannock had slammed earlier.

There was only one real contender—just four seconds'

walk along the corridor. Chance turned the jammer back on, marched up to the door and knocked on it loudly.

"Come on, come on," he growled in his best approximation of an angry Scottish accent.

The door started to open. Chance kicked it as hard as he could. The door flew back, catching the man holding it a nasty crack on the chin. He fell backward with a cry and lay still on the floor.

A second man was getting to his feet from an armchair in front of a large dark wood desk. His hand was inside his jacket pocket. But before he could draw his gun, Chance was across the room, swatting the man with his briefcase. There was an unpleasant crunch of bone and the man fell to the floor.

Chance looked around the room, but no one else was there. He swore quietly. This had to be the room—the presence of the guards confirmed it. Had they moved the "property"?

He had another minute, perhaps two at most, before Bannock came back. He couldn't turn off the jammer again as there were sure to be cameras in this room—it looked like the manager's office. Plush carpet, big desk, paneled walls and a large abstract painting that reached almost from floor to ceiling and that you could bet concealed a big safe.

Safe.

Chance pulled at the frame of the painting. It swung back and revealed a solid metal door. Probably the most secure safe to be found in this part of the world, Chance thought. And he had at most a minute.

It took him forty-five seconds, with his ear pressed to an

upturned glass from the desk as he listened for the click of the tumblers. Then the last one clicked into place and Chance swung open the heavy reinforced steel door.

A small frightened man with thinning gray hair stared out of the dark safe, blinking through round, pebble-lensed glasses.

Chance opened the briefcase and the man cowered away, back into the safe.

"It's okay," Chance told him. "Ardman sent me. I'm here to help you, not kill you. Now . . ." He pulled out the suit, the wig and the false beard. "You've got about twenty seconds to get these on."

An unremarkable man of about forty walked nonchalantly out of the casino and down the steps toward a waiting car. With him was an older, smaller man who seemed nervous. Whereas the younger man was clean shaven, the older man had a mass of dark curly hair and a bushy beard that almost completely concealed his features.

The first man paused to hand a couple of casino chips to the doorman and share a quick joke about easy money. The doorman wasn't to know the chips had been in the casino safe just a minute earlier. The bearded man seemed impatient to be on his way.

The car was a silver Mercedes—big, fast, expensive. John Chance opened the back door to allow the man with the wig and false beard to climb inside with an audible sigh of relief.

The driver rolled down the window. "Where to, guv'nor?"

he asked in a mock Cockney accent, imitating a London cabdriver.

"Don't overdo it, Dex," Chance said. Dex Halford was an old friend from his SAS days—the two of them had worked together more times than either cared to remember. "They let you drive with just one leg, do they?"

Halford gave a short laugh and slapped his leg. It was false from below the knee. "Car's automatic," he told Chance. "Though sadly, I still have to be here to steer it."

"Yes, well, I think it's time you weren't," Chance told Halford.

"Problems?"

Chance shook his head. "Piece of cake. But tell Ardman that from now on, I really am on holiday. If he wants anything else done, he can—" His words were drowned out by the strident sound of alarm bells from inside the casino.

"Enjoy the death run," he shouted over the noise. Chance saw sudden fear and anxiety in the eyes of the small man in the backseat. "Don't worry—that's what we call this. When you get whisked away to a new life, a new identity. When you disappear forever. The death run."

"I'll take good care of you, no fear," Halford told the man. "Say hi to the family," he told Chance.

Chance slapped his hand on the roof of the car as Halford closed the window. The car screeched away and headed off into the night.

Chance watched the taillights disappear into the darkness. Then he turned to the casino. The big Scotsman,

Bannock, was on the steps, looking around in fury and confusion. Behind him, Chance could see men in suits running back and forth. A woman with long auburn hair wearing a pale blue evening dress sipped her champagne and watched it all with amusement. For a moment her startling blue eyes locked with Chance's. But he wasn't interested.

He looked up at a window on the side of the casino. The window next to his own bedroom. Curtains billowed out over the balcony and two young faces looked down at him—both blond, a boy and a girl. They didn't look pleased.

Chance headed quickly back into the casino, walking confidently through the noise and confusion toward the stairs of the hotel. He clicked off the jammer in his pocket and smiled at a man shouting urgently into a radio.

"Now for the tricky bit," Chance murmured as he headed back to face Rich and Jade.

It was hot and humid in Venice in the last week of August. One canal looked pretty much like another to Jade, the churches all looked the same and the whole place smelled old and damp. It was probably better than hanging around in London with nothing to do till school started again, but if she had to eat any more pasta or gelato, Jade reckoned there would be serious trouble.

As usual, it was difficult to know what Dad thought of it all. But since he'd brought them here, he was presumably enjoying himself. They stayed in a small family-run hotel close to the Grand Canal. It amused Jade that the bar closed at nine in the evening and if Dad wanted a drink after that, he had to find the night porter.

Rich seemed to be enjoying himself. He greeted every new street or stretch of water, every café and old building with excitement. "Have you seen this?" he exclaimed with interest as they turned into a small square close to the canal.

"Oh yeah, look," Jade muttered back. "Another church.

Well, who'd have thought." But she had to smile at his enthusiasm.

"Yeah, but they're all different," Rich told her. "I mean, talk about paintings!"

"You do that a lot," she pointed out.

"Only takes a few minutes to look around," Dad said. "We should do it while we're here."

"I suppose."

There was a small café opposite. Dad suggested they take a look in the church, then stop for a drink.

She didn't like to admit it, but Jade found it refreshingly cool inside the church. There were indeed paintings—several small icons and an ornamental screen. The paintings were dark with age, but Rich was fascinated.

"Are we having fun yet?" Dad said quietly to Jade.

"I suppose," she admitted.

"I'll take that as a yes, then." He smiled at her, and she couldn't help but smile back.

"It's fine, Dad. Great. Church, paintings, everything." Jade's smile widened into a grin. "Can we go now?"

They were getting toward the end of their stay in Venice, and Jade had found herself relaxing into the slow pace of the holiday. Perhaps she was adapting to the ways of the city. Or perhaps it was the heat. But by their last couple of days, Jade was as happy as her brother and father to sit outside the small café and let the day go by.

"I think that woman is following us," Rich said quietly as

he drank his Coke. Jade had ordered mineral water, while Dad had an espresso that was thick as syrup.

"Describe her," Dad said at once, not looking around. Jade glanced where Rich was looking, then away again, pretending to be admiring the small square they were in. It was just like a hundred other small squares they'd been to.

"Tall, slim. Smartly dressed. Long hair that's a sort of auburn color. I'm sure the same woman was a couple of tables away from us at dinner last night."

Dad frowned. "Sounds like a woman I noticed the other day in the casino."

"So you *were* in the casino?" Jade said.

"I mean the hotel. At the casino. I told you—I heard the alarms and nipped down to see what was happening."

"Climbing out the window and down the wall?" Jade pointed out.

Dad shrugged. "Force of habit. Anyway, it was a lot of fuss about nothing. False alarm or something. And it's probably a completely different woman. Just a coincidence."

"What if it isn't?" Rich asked. "What if she's . . . I don't know, an agent or something?"

Jade laughed at that. "More likely she's a tourist. If we go to the obvious boring touristy places, we're going to see some of the same obvious boring tourists, aren't we?"

Dad drained his coffee and pushed a few euros under the saucer to pay the bill. "Easy enough to find out."

"So what's the plan?" Jade asked.

"Well, you're complaining you're bored, Jade—what do you want to do for the rest of the afternoon?" Chance asked.

"Not churches," Jade said at once. "There was that little street of decent shops you wouldn't let us stop at yesterday."

"Because we're here on holiday, not to buy new sneakers and T-shirts," Rich reminded them.

"Okay," Dad said. "And you, Rich?"

"I'm happy to wander. Browse the shops a bit. Are we splitting up?"

Dad nodded. "We'll see if that woman follows any of us. I'll go first and double back around so I can follow her."

"Sneaky," Rich said. "But what if she follows you?"

"She won't. She won't realize I'm leaving." As he spoke, Dad stood up. "Meet back here in an hour, okay?"

"Okay," they both agreed.

Dad walked slowly, almost lazily into the café. Jade risked another quick look at the woman. She was reading a book, maybe a guidebook—a small paperback. She didn't seem to have reacted to Dad leaving the table. But then she was probably expecting him to come back and for all three of them to leave together.

"You really think she's following us?" Jade asked.

Rich shrugged. "We'll soon know."

Jade grinned. "If she is, I reckon it's just because she fancies Dad."

Rich shuddered at the thought. "That's so gross."

They stood up together, then headed off in opposite directions out of the little square. If the woman with the auburn hair noticed, she gave no sign.

After ten minutes, Rich was bored of wandering around on his own. He considered returning to the café, but that might spoil whatever Dad was up to. So instead he went looking for Jade. He remembered the street where she'd wanted to look at the designer clothes and sports stuff.

It was only a few minutes' walk. Rich paused on a steep-backed, narrow bridge over a canal and admired the view. He liked the way the water and the streets seemed to exist in harmony. The tall, square buildings emerging from the water made everything seem even more narrow and closed in.

He found Jade in the second shop he tried. She was trying on running shoes but hadn't found any she liked. Jade was picky when it came to running shoes. Actually, Rich thought, she was picky about most things.

"Find any good churches, then?" Jade asked as they walked slowly back along the street.

Rich shook his head. "Nothing worth mentioning."

"There's some weird stuff here," Jade said. She paused outside what seemed to be an antiques shop. "I mean, look at all that."

There were several chess sets in the window, laid out on marble boards. One of them was made of gold, and the tag hanging from the side of the board looked more like a telephone number than a price. On each side of the window display stood a figure, as if they were keeping guard. One was a woman in a brightly colored, flowing dress. The mannequin's face was a smooth, white mask with a peacock painted on it in brilliant blue. Dark holes for the eyes formed part of the feathers of the peacock.

"That's beautiful," Jade said in surprise.

"That isn't," said Rich, pointing at the other figure. "It's grotesque."

The second figure was a man. He wore long, dark robes and held a stick as if it was a magic wand. His face too was a mask—but a plain, gray mask that jutted out like an enormous cruel beak. The only color in the mask was the black outline of a pair of spectacles around the eyes.

"Who are they supposed to be?" Jade wondered.

"I don't know, but I wouldn't want to meet them outside of a shop display."

2

Once inside the café, John Chance asked if there was a back way out. There was, out past the waste bins and down a tiny alleyway alongside a canal. He made his way rapidly, ignoring the smell from the bins, and emerged into a side street just off the back of the square.

It took him only a minute to double back and approach the square from a different direction. He hesitated at the edge of the square, looking for the young woman Rich had described. He had taken a moment to case her out from inside the café—and it was definitely the woman he had noticed at the casino. A coincidence? It was possible, but highly unlikely. So who was she, and why was she following him?

But the table where the woman had been was empty. He would not get the answer to his questions just yet. Chance walked slowly around the square, looking along each of the streets leading off it in turn. There was no sign of the woman with auburn hair. Satisfied that, for now at least, he was not being watched, Chance returned to the table outside the café.

He'd had enough coffee for today, so he ordered a carafe of white wine.

He was halfway through it when Rich and Jade returned.

"So?" Jade asked as she sat down. She glanced disapprovingly at the wine. It was barely lunchtime and he'd started already. Still, at least he wasn't smoking.

"Yeah, what happened to your girlfriend?" Rich asked.

Dad took a pack of cigarettes out of his shirt pocket. "She didn't wait for me to introduce myself. I wondered if she'd followed either of you?"

"Not that we noticed," Jade said. "You're not going to smoke that, are you?" She was glaring at the cigarette between Dad's fingers.

"No, I'm going to juggle with it."

"Funny man."

Dad pushed the cigarette back into the pack. He was getting better, Jade had to admit. He did actually seem to listen to what she and Rich said. That was a distinct improvement.

"Speaking of jugglers," Dad was saying. "What's with the fancy dress party?"

Rich gasped, and Jade turned quickly to see what he and Dad were looking at.

It was like the shop display had come to life and followed them. A small group of half a dozen men was walking slowly into the little square from one of the side streets. They were all wearing dark business suits, and all had their faces covered by masks. The man at the front was wearing a savagely beaked gray face—just like in the display.

Behind him came two men in golden gargoyle masks, then a man whose face was completely white except for a single black teardrop on one cheek. Another of them was Harlequin—like the joker from a deck of cards, a black and red face with spikes springing from his head.

The last man wore the blank-eyed grinning face of a skull. Jade shuddered. If this was someone's idea of fun, it was pretty bizarre. And why wear heavy, dark clothes in this heat?

"Some sort of parade," Dad said. "Wrong time of year for Carnival."

Rich looked at Jade, and she saw how pale he was. "I don't like this."

"Me neither," she agreed. At first she'd thought, like Dad, that it was a bit of fun. Some sort of parade. Now Jade was sure it wasn't. There was something sinister about the figures—about the way they moved, the way they had paused just inside the square. They slowly swung around, as if looking for something. Or someone. They all stopped at the same point—staring directly at Jade, Rich and their father.

Dad's chair scraped backward on the flagstones as he stood up. "Wait for me back at the hotel."

"What are you going to do?" Jade asked.

"I don't know. Get moving."

"We can't leave you," Rich said. The men were walking

slowly across the square toward them. The beak of the gray mask was aimed directly at Dad.

"Move it!" Dad urged. "And don't worry. I'll probably overtake you."

Jade grabbed Rich's hand and together they ran from the square.

"We can't leave him with them," Rich gasped as they ran.

"What do you suggest?"

"We have to see what's happening." Rich slowed to a jog and Jade eased up as well. "We should go back."

"That's probably what they want."

"So what—do nothing?"

"No." Jade pointed to a small alleyway between two buildings. "If we cut through there, we can get back to the square on a different street. They won't expect that."

"You hope."

"All right, Einstein—let's hear your idea."

Rich sighed. "Let's try the alley," he conceded.

Dad was talking to the man in the gray, beaked mask. He was shaking his head, turning away. Then the masked man said something that Jade and Rich couldn't hear, but they heard their father laugh. He waved a hand as if dismissing whatever the masked man had said. Then he held up a finger—a "back in a minute" gesture—and walked into the café.

"He's all right," Jade realized. "He'll leg it out the back, like before."

"If they fall for it."

It didn't look like they had. The gray-masked man was gesturing to the two golden gargoyles, who ran after Dad into the café. Moments later there were shouts from inside and the other masked men followed in a hurry.

"I expect he'll be all right," Jade said.

"Course he will." Rich sounded more confident than Jade felt. "Think we should help him?"

"How? Come on, let's get back to the hotel like Dad said."

"And hope he meets us there."

It wasn't far, and walking briskly, they were back in half an hour. It probably wasn't the quickest route—Rich had led them back the same way as they had come that morning. At least they didn't stop at every church this time.

"You wait here," Rich told Jade as they walked through the little foyer into the small lounge bar. "I'll check he's not already back in his room. Anyone who knows the way could be here before us."

Jade slumped down on a sofa. It wasn't as comfortable as it looked, but she settled into it and watched the door. A large black car bumped up the narrow cobbled street outside and stopped opposite the hotel. No one got out, and Jade frowned. It was unusual to see a car right in the heart of Venice. For one thing, the streets weren't really wide enough. She was about to run up the stairs after Rich when she heard his scream.

Rich took the stairs two at a time. The door to their room was standing open, and he sighed with relief. He went straight in, not thinking it might be a trap.

As soon as he was through the door, everything went black. He had time to cry out in surprise and alarm—just once. Then he was fighting against the blanket that was tight over his face and shoulders. Rich was being dragged out of the room and back down the stairs. His feet caught on the threadbare carpet and knocked painfully against the wall of the stairwell as he was bundled away.

Soon he was on level ground again, the thin lounge carpet under his feet. Then he heard his feet scrape on the bare stone floor of the lobby, followed by the warm breeze on his hands and a brightness even through the blanket. He was struggling to speak, but his throat was clogged with dust and whenever he tried, he ended up coughing and choking. There were uneven cobbles under his feet now. His head was pushed roughly down and he was shoved forward—landing on something soft. A chair? Where was he?

An engine revved. A door slammed. Rich was in a car, and it was pulling away.

Jade emerged from behind the sofa. She'd been ready to fight the men to get Rich free. But a glance from her hiding place at the four men in Carnival masks had been enough to tell her it was no use. She'd end up being captured herself. It made her sick to her stomach, but the best option was to leave Rich to fend for himself.

At least he wouldn't be on his own—Jade would follow. But then she saw Rich bundled into the car opposite the hotel and her heart sank still lower. She couldn't follow a car.

But she'd try. She wouldn't give up and abandon her brother. Jade was out of the hotel and running after the car as it started up the street. She kept to the shadowed side of the pavement, hoping they wouldn't spot her. Mercifully, the dark limousine was going quite slowly up the uneven street. And Jade ran every day. If it kept to this speed, she might—just might—keep it in sight.

The car reached the end of the street and turned right. Almost immediately it turned again—toward the main street. Jade hesitated. Should she follow, or should she take a risk? She'd lose the car if she just followed. She'd risk it, she decided—take a shortcut she'd discovered along an alley and over a little canal bridge. That would bring her to the same junction as the car was making for. *Probably* making for . . .

At the junction, Jade paused for breath. There was no sign of the car. It couldn't have got here already. But after almost a minute, Jade realized it wasn't coming. It was too distinctive for her to have missed. She'd gambled and lost. The car had not been heading for the main road at all.

With a shout of frustration, Jade turned and kicked the wall of the building behind her.

The car stopped abruptly and Rich was thrown forward in the seat. Someone laughed as he collided with the back of the seat in front. Then the door opened and he was hauled out. If they didn't take the blanket off soon, he'd suffocate. That is, if he didn't die of fright first—he could feel himself shaking. What was going on?

Indoors again. It sounded large—echoey. Even through the blanket the place smelled old.

Suddenly the blanket was pulled off his head and Rich spluttered and coughed as he rasped for breath. The room was dim and barely lit, but he blinked at the relative brightness of it.

A golden gargoyle face was close in front of his own—so close his breath misted its cheek as Rich gasped and tried to pull away. Then the mask was pulled off, just as Rich's blanket had been. A man with short black hair and a neat pencil mustache stared at Rich through disbelieving eyes and let loose a tirade of rapid Italian.

Rich didn't understand a word of it, but it didn't sound polite.

Then, in English, "You are not Chance!"

"I am," Rich retorted, trying to sound confident and in control. "Richard Chance." And he gave a short laugh as he realized what had happened. Despite everything, it was almost funny. The laugh made him cough, and he gasped for breath again. "You were after Dad, weren't you? You just assumed he'd come back to the hotel, and as soon as someone came in, you stuffed a blanket over them and bundled them off. Sorry." He paused for another cough and was pleased to find his throat was easing a little. "You took a chance and got the wrong Chance."

The Italian stared back at Rich. He didn't look at all happy. Maybe Rich shouldn't have laughed at him, but it was too late now. The man stepped back and snarled something at the others. Two of them grabbed Rich roughly by the shoulders and dragged him deeper into the old building.

Jade's foot hurt. She had no one to blame but herself—for everything. She limped slowly along the pavement, walking back the way she had expected the car to come. It must have turned off somewhere between the junction and where she had last seen it.

Five minutes later, she turned a corner and saw the car parked at the curb. The whole area was run-down and dilapidated. The walls of the buildings were crumbling and cracked. The cobblestones were split or missing. In the gap between the buildings Jade could see the sunlight reflecting off the water of a canal. The dark shape of a gondola drifted by, blotting out the sunlight for a moment.

The building that the car was parked outside looked like it had once been grand and impressive. Flaking remains of gold leaf clung to weathered stone ornamentation around the entrance. The door was a rotting apology of damp wood. It creaked and complained as Jade eased it open. She stood for a moment, half expecting shouts and running men to respond to the noise. But there was nothing.

Was this the right place? Or had they just abandoned the car and gone somewhere else?

Jade went inside, pausing to allow her eyes to adjust to the lack of light. She was in a large entrance lobby. There was a booth on one side, steps leading up to a raised area at the back and then doors off to the side. It took Jade a moment to realize where she was.

She was in the lobby of a theater. Slowly and quietly, Jade climbed the steps. The main doors were chained shut. She gave the chain a tug, feeling the rust rubbing away on her palm. But it was secure. A side door led to a flight of steps that swept around and up impressively. Except the carpet was worn through, and the heavy rope handrails were rotten and frayed.

Jade emerged into the upper circle of the theater. She made her way quietly down to the front seats to get the best view of what was happening on the stage. The theater might be old and disused, neglected and in need of repair, but on the stage were four men. Three of them were in Carnival masks. All of them were standing around a fifth figure tied to a chair. The chair was facing away from Jade, toward the decaying backdrop of the stage—a faded painting of mountains and a castle. But even so, she knew who it was—she recognized the profile and the tousled blond hair.

"Oh, Rich." She sighed.

The man dressed as Harlequin turned to look up at the circle—at Jade. She ducked down quickly. Had her words carried right to the front of the theater? She risked a look over the low wall at the front of the circle. Harlequin had turned away again, but Jade knew she had better be very, very quiet.

But the sound carried both ways, she realized, as the man who had removed his mask spoke. "Don't worry. It won't be long now."

"What won't?" Jade could hear how nervous and frightened

Rich was, though he was trying to hide it. "What are you going to do to me? Why don't you just let me go—it's not me you want."

"But you may be useful." The man's English was perfect; only a slight accent gave away that he was Italian. "And anyway, it is not for me to decide."

"Then who?"

"The boss is coming. The big man." He laughed, and the sound echoed around the damp walls of the old theater. "Dr. Plague will decide what to do with you. I wonder, what will be the treatment? Kill or cure?"

The men all laughed at that. Jade gritted her teeth. Keeping low, kneeling on the floor in the aisle beside the front row of seats, Jade eased her cell phone out of her pocket. She checked it was set to silent and selected SEND SHORT MESSAGE from the main menu.

They got Rich. Old Theater. Come help.

She hoped Dad had his phone on. She hoped he knew what to do if he got a text message—Mum had never understood how her cell worked apart from the phone bit. Jade wiped her eyes on the back of her sleeve as she waited. She couldn't help feeling upset as she thought about Mum—and about Rich tied to a chair on the stage far below.

The phone trembled in her hand. It took her a moment to realize it wasn't just her hand shaking with emotion. She had a text, thank God!

What old theater?

Jade stared at the message. Then she sent back:

Dunno

A moment later she got:

OK. What street?

She almost yelled at the phone. Instead she clenched her mouth tight shut and sent back:

Dunno

A pause, then:

So what's near it?

Jade stared at the phone. She tried to think how she had got here, which turns and side streets she had taken from the junction with the main road, but she just couldn't picture it. All she could think of was the light reflecting off the water glimpsed between the buildings outside.

Er—a canal

She could only guess how Dad would react to that. She sent another text; it wasn't much, but it was the best she could do:

Something was happening on the stage below. The four men were stepping back as others arrived. Two people—both in masks. The skull man and the man in the gray, beak-faced mask stepped up onto the stage.

The skull man pulled off his mask, and Jade was startled to see that underneath, his face looked very much the same—white teeth between bloodless lips and skin stretched tight and thin over a pale, bald head. The man's cheekbones jutted out prominently.

"What have we here?" he asked in a voice that also sounded stretched and thin. "This is not John Chance," he said angrily, turning to the gray-masked man. "Dr. Plague?!" he demanded.

Dr. Plague turned slowly toward Rich. There was a rumble of sound from behind the mask—exaggerated and distorted by the beaked shape of the mask. But the sound was unmistakable.

Dr. Plague was laughing.

3

The sound of laughter echoed inside Dr. Plague's mask. "This is the ever-resourceful young Rich."

His voice was a rumble amplified by the mask's beak-like shape—but still, Jade could tell that his accent was different from the other man's. There was something oddly familiar about his voice, in fact. But the man's next words made Jade's heart skip a beat. He stepped in front of Rich and said, "How nice to see you again, my friend."

Jade leaned forward. The man was facing her. She struggled to make out any features behind the mask. But there was nothing. Until the man reached up and took off the mask to reveal the distinctive weathered face behind. He had dark, thinning hair and a thin, neatly trimmed mustache.

"Ralph!" Rich's exclamation masked the sound of Jade's gasp of surprise.

Like Rich, she knew the man—knew him as Ralph, though she also knew that was not his real name. They had met in the former Soviet state of Krejikistan when he had helped

Jade and Rich rescue their dad from the mad oil baron Viktor Vishinsky. What was a powerful Eastern European gangster doing in Venice?

"After our mutual friend Mr. Vishinsky was no longer 'available,'" Ralph was saying, "most of his assets fell into my hands. I have a lot to thank you for."

"Is that why you brought me here?" Rich asked defiantly. "Well, thanks accepted. No problem. So you've become public enemy number one in Krejikistan or whatever. And grown a neat mustache to prove it. Can I go now?"

Ralph laughed and wagged his finger like a teacher warning a small child. "I am afraid there is a little more to it than that."

"I was afraid there might be." Rich looked up at Ralph, his face set. "Are you going to kill me?"

Ralph looked offended. "Oh, please. We are all friends here. You, me, your family. And speaking of family . . ." He spread his hands to include the men in suits. "My Italian colleagues too. We just want to talk to your father about some work he did in Mont Passat."

Rich shook his head. "He didn't do any work in Mont Passat. We were only there for a day. Not even that."

"Oh, Rich, Rich, Rich." Ralph shook his head in amusement. "Now, we both know that just isn't true."

Jade didn't hear Rich's answer. She needed to get closer so she could rescue him if she got the opportunity. Though Ralph had helped them before, she knew only too well that the man was a criminal—he'd told them himself that whatever he did was for his own good, in his own interests. For his own survival.

She edged her way carefully back toward the stairs. As she went, she dialed Dad on her cell. He answered at once and she whispered urgently into the phone—telling him as best she could where she was.

"I'm on it," Dad told her. "I'll find you. Just sit tight and wait till I get there, right?"

"What's going on?" Jade asked quietly. "You spoke to Ralph—what's he after?"

"He said he wanted to talk. I told him I was on vacation. End of story."

"Except they got Rich," Jade pointed out. "I'll try and get closer. I'll leave the phone on so you can hear. But Dad . . ." Her voice trailed off as she headed down a corridor that ran along the back of the circle, leading—she hoped—closer to the stage.

"Don't worry," he said. "I'll hurry."

The first door that Jade tried opened into a box almost alongside the stage. It was so close that the curtain that hung down at the side of the stage almost touched the side of the box. It was faded, torn and filthy.

Jade crept forward, keeping low, hidden by the front wall of the box and shadowed by the way the curtain hung. The seats were worn and the fabric ripped. Jade perched on the front of the cleanest looking and stared down at the stage. She could see Rich's profile and Ralph standing talking to him.

The men had all taken their masks off now. Ralph was the

shortest of them, but standing with his hands clasped in front of him as he spoke to Rich, he was easily the most impressive and powerful figure on the stage. Obviously in charge.

"So what's with the masks and the Dr. Plague stuff?" Rich was asking.

"They are costumes for Carnival," Ralph explained. "Some are just for decoration, to look pretty." He gestured to the Harlequin man at the edge of the stage. "Others, like Harlequin, are from the *commedia dell'arte*. Characters from the plays."

"And what about you?" Rich asked. "Dr. Plague—who's that?"

"When the plague came to Venice in medieval times, the doctors wore a black gown and a mask like this to protect themselves from the disease."

Forget dying of the plague, Jade thought as she crouched in the box above the stage. *He would probably scare his patients to death.* She was focused on Ralph as he nodded to one of the Italians. "Family" he had called them—Mafia. Jade leaned forward, keeping in the shadows cast by the dusty ragged curtain.

"The business of crime is money," Ralph said. "Large amounts of money, one hopes. And like any business, it has to be accounted for."

"So?" Rich asked.

"So the actual accountancy is quite involved. There are so many expenses, so many people on the payroll. Pension schemes of a sort. Profit and, sadly, loss."

"So get an accountant."

"Oh, I have an accountant. The very best accountant. A man who is both accountant and banker. He is Swiss, of course. The very best in his business. He borrows my money and lends it to others at a good rate of interest. He is a very clever man. Banker to so very many people in my line of work as well as dozens of more legitimate businesses. I really cannot afford to do without him . . ."

"And why are you telling me this?"

Ralph walked quickly across the stage to Rich. He put his hand on Rich's shoulder and leaned down to look at him closely. "Because several days ago, I heard rumors that my banker was planning to defect. To give himself up to the authorities and hand over access to a large number of accounts he controls. In return for immunity, anonymity, a new secret life.

"Now, I wasn't the only person who heard these rumors. There is another man—a very unpleasant man who deals in matters that even I would think twice about—who also heard. And he decided he would have a word with the Banker and see if there was any truth in the rumors. This man, who is known only as the Tiger, funds all sorts of unpleasantness—crime and murder and terrorism. He invests and he clears a profit. And the Banker controls almost all his money. So you see, he had a lot to lose. Now, then—I think it's time for a little show. This is, after all, a theater."

A bright light snapped on, shining above Rich onto the faded backdrop like a spotlight. Ralph's elongated shadow seemed to be standing at the gates of a painted castle. He walked quickly to the side of the stage so as not to be in the way. Then he straightened up and clicked his fingers. On cue, a picture appeared on the backdrop, and Jade realized the light was from a projector somewhere up in the main part of the theater. The picture showed the hotel and casino where they had stayed just a few nights ago.

"The Tiger had the Banker taken to Mont Passat. But before he could get there himself to question the man . . . the Banker disappeared."

"And what's that got to do with us?"

Jade could hear a hesitancy in her brother's voice. She could guess what he was thinking.

The picture on the backdrop changed to grainy moving images—pictures from a security camera complete with time and date stamp on the bottom. The footage showed the inside of a casino. It panned back and forth, taking in most of the gaming floor.

"This is from the CCTV in the casino on the night the Banker vanished," Ralph was saying.

At the edge of its journey, the camera swung past a bar. And standing at the bar, drink in hand, was their dad.

"And look who is also there. What a coincidence," Ralph said in feigned surprise.

"It must be," Rich said. But he didn't sound very sure.

"And if we continue on a bit . . ." Ralph waved to the man working the projector and the images sped up—people hurrying and scurrying around the casino floor. "Oh—look," Ralph went on as the footage slowed back to normal speed.

It showed Dad at the roulette table. Placing a bet.

"You getting this, are you?" Jade whispered into the phone, ducking behind the front of the box. "Because when you get here, you are *so* in trouble."

"It doesn't mean anything," Rich was saying. He sounded less certain than ever now. "It *could* be a coincidence. Just a coincidence."

"Really?" Ralph sighed. He clicked his fingers again and the projector cut off. "I suppose it could. But neither of us really believes that, do we?"

Jade was angry as well as frightened now. But never mind what the hell Dad had been up to. It was time to get Rich away from here.

At that moment, the insistent sound of a car alarm came from close outside. On the stage below, Ralph was talking rapidly to the man with the skull face. He gestured urgently, and the five Italians hurried toward the front of the theater.

"Probably nothing," Ralph said to Rich. "But it is as well to be sure. And we would, after all, like your father to come looking for you. You see, I have a warning to deliver to him."

She wasn't going to get a better opportunity than this—only Ralph was left with Rich on the stage below. Jade heard the main theater doors bang shut as the others left. She grabbed hold of the ragged curtain hanging down the side of the stage, swung her legs up and over the side of the box and began to climb down.

Jade could feel the material breaking apart under her hands, could hear an ominous creaking sound from above. She descended as fast as she could, half sliding down and sending out clouds of dust—desperate not to cough as she breathed in, desperate for Ralph *not* to look up and see her.

A patter of dust sprinkled across Ralph's shoulders. He looked up.

At the same moment, the curtain began to tear. Jade could hear the threads ripping apart. She felt the curtain fall, jolt to a stop, then start to fall again. She was accelerating rapidly as the material ripped under her weight.

"Jade!" Rich shouted.

Ralph was staring up at her in surprise.

Then the curtain gave way entirely and Jade was falling.

Ralph gave a cry of realization. But it was too late—Jade fell right on top of him. Her feet cannoned into the man's bulky form and sent him sprawling backward. Jade was on her feet at once, running to where Rich was tied to the chair. She tugged at the knots.

Several meters away, Ralph struggled to his feet. Then a massive moth-eaten theater curtain landed on him, burying him in dusty, ragged material.

"Come on!" Jade yelled as she finally pried apart the last knot.

The curtain heaved as Ralph tried to get out from under it. His hand clawed through the decayed fabric, clutching at the air. In a moment, he'd be out and free.

"Thanks. That was pretty neat," Rich gasped as they ran for the back of the stage.

"That was pretty scary," Jade admitted.

Rich was grinning. "Looked it. There must be a back way out of here."

Behind the stage was a corridor. They sprinted along it, Rich rubbing at his sore wrists, Jade punching Dad's number into her phone. At the end of the corridor was a fire door. As they approached, it sprang open.

"Back the other way!" yelled Rich.

But Jade skidded to a halt. "No—wait." She could hear a phone ringing. "It's Dad!"

And sure enough, Dad appeared in the doorway. "Quick. Someone vandalized their car, but they'll be back soon."

"Wonder who that was," Rich said as they emerged, blinking, into the bright sunlight beside a narrow canal.

"Same guy who lied about drinking, gambling and kidnapping in Mont Passat," Jade said.

"Not fair. It was a rescue, not a kidnap," Chance protested.

"Whatever," Jade said.

"Later!" Rich yelled at them both.

At the same moment, there was another shout. The skull-faced man had appeared down the side of the theater ahead of them. He was holding a gun.

"Later," Jade agreed.

The other Mafia men were close behind Skull Face. They didn't look happy. Rich, Jade and their dad turned and ran. Ahead of them, the pavement ended in a small wooden dock. Beyond that was the canal. They were trapped.

4

"I am *not* swimming," Rich said. "That water's filthy!"

"Not a lot of choice," Jade told him.

"There's always a choice," Dad shot back. He was in the lead, running full steam across the dock—heading straight for the canal. And when he got to the edge, he kept running.

Rich was waiting for the splash, but as they reached the edge of the dock, he could hear Dad yelling at them to hurry up. Somehow—impossibly—Dad was standing on a narrow strip of pathway farther along the canal. He looked completely dry.

Three strides onto the wooden dock and Rich could see what he'd done. There was a line of five gondolas moored next to the dock—a bridge across to where Dad was standing. Except the gondolas were bobbing in the water and there was a gap of a meter or more between each.

The boards were wobbling under their feet, but Rich and Jade ran faster—right to the edge of the dock. And jumped.

"Oh, my God!" Rich said. His foot jarred painfully as it hit the bottom of the first boat. The gondola heaved beneath him and he almost fell. Water in the bottom of the shallow boat washed over his shoes. Jade clutched at him as she landed too. They both leaped for the next in the line.

Again it was a jarring moment as they landed. But immediately they were on to the next. Rich could hear the thump of heavy footsteps on the wooden dock behind them. He did not look back.

On the third gondola, Jade sprawled forward and Rich grabbed her, dragging her to her feet. He was breathing heavily. "Nearly there."

"You think?"

Rich turned to see what she meant. There were two more gondolas to go. The next one was decked out with garlands of white flowers. A black coffin lay in the middle of it—right in their path. On the middle of the coffin, there was a single wet footprint.

"Oh, great," said Rich. He took Jade's hand and together they jumped again.

The coffin was polished and slippery, and Rich felt his foot slide from under him. He pushed off as best he could. But he knew at once that he wasn't going to make it across the next gap. The final gondola was moving. It wasn't moored like the others—there was a man in black trousers and a striped shirt sitting back in the boat close to the single large oar. He was staring in openmouthed astonishment at Rich and Jade as they flailed in the air.

The gondolier grabbed the oar and heaved hard. The boat swung sideways. Somehow Rich was almost on it. His foot caught the side and he was flung forward into the boat. His wrist cracked painfully on the side of the boat. Jade landed heavily beside him. A moment later two large, heavy feet landed squarely between them. A familiar voice shouted in Italian at the gondolier.

Dad hauled Rich and Jade to their feet. "Good idea," he said.

The gondolier was on his feet now and working the oar like his life depended on it. Maybe Dad had told him that it did. The gondola moved surprisingly fast through the water. The skull-faced man was on the boat next to them and, with a shout of rage, launched himself across the canal straight at Rich.

Again the gondolier heaved sideways on the oar. Skull Face landed on the boat, and the whole gondola tipped under his weight. The gondolier heaved again, and Skull Face, off balance from his landing, staggered backward. He fell over the side with a stream of angry Italian followed by a loud splash.

"Oh, yuck!" Jade wiped her sleeve across her wet face.

The gondolier laughed and shouted something to Dad, who laughed back. "*Grazie*, Giuseppe," he said.

"You know him?" Rich asked in surprise. He rubbed at his wrist, annoyed to see the impact had cracked the glass of his watch.

"I do now," Chance said.

Two angry men in suits were standing on the dock watching them as the gondola moved away. A third was helping Skull Face out of the water into one of the moored gondolas.

"Where are the others?" Jade wondered.

"Well, it was curtains for Ralph," Rich said. "Don't know about the other guy."

"I do," Dad said. He was pointing to a steeply arched bridge in front of them. On it stood a tall, thin man in a dark suit. Next to him was Ralph, slowly clapping.

"I think you can drop us just here, Giuseppe," Dad said to the gondolier, indicating a point at the side of the canal before the bridge.

But Ralph and the Mafia man with him had realized where they were heading and were already running from the bridge.

Dad thrust a few euro notes at the gondolier as they all three leaped off.

"Keep the change," Rich told him.

The point where the Grand Canal doubles back on itself is called the Volta. Cutting between high, impressive buildings, Chance and the twins found that they were in the area inside the curve of the canal.

"This way," Dad yelled, leading them between yet more buildings.

They passed a line of garbage cans, and Jade paused to pull several over. Dead flowers and old chicken bones strewed across the passageway, but the cans themselves would slow down their pursuers.

Rich could hear Ralph shouting somewhere behind them. "We need to lose ourselves in the crowds!" he said. The heat was getting to him, and sweat was running down his face.

"Yeah, what crowds?" Jade was right—the narrow side streets were almost deserted.

"We'll find some," Dad promised. "San Marco is this way. Loads of people."

They emerged into yet another small square. There was a church on one side, a small shop on the other. The store's window was full of colorful Murano glass—vases and bottles, ornaments and figures.

"If we get that far," Jade said.

There were two other streets leading off the square. Two of the men in suits were coming down one of the streets. The skull-faced man, soaking wet, and another of his Mafia colleagues were coming down the other.

"Back the way we came?" Rich suggested.

But as they turned, Ralph and the man who had been with him on the bridge appeared around the corner behind them. Rich wondered if they could get to the church and find another way out. But Skull Face was already too close—they'd never make it.

"Let's go shopping," Dad said quietly. Then louder: "Now!"

They sprinted to the shop doorway and dashed inside. The shop was full of expensive glassware, all arranged on shelves and pedestals. There were statues and vases, ornaments and sculptures. Dad was reeling off rapid Italian to a little old lady standing behind a low counter that boasted a cash register and a roll of floral wrapping paper. Without a word, she pointed to the back of the shop.

"*Grazie,*" said Dad.

"*Ciao,*" Rich told her.

There was a door at the back of the shop and Dad barged through it. He held it open for Rich and Jade, then slammed it shut. They were in a small courtyard.

"Hang on," Jade said. She grabbed a long-handled broom that was leaning against a wall and jammed it hard against the door. It wouldn't keep Ralph and the others in for long, but it might slow them down.

From the other side of the door came the sound of smashing glass—lots of glass. Then furious cursing in a high-pitched female voice, followed by a man's cries of pain.

"Maybe she's got another broom in there," Rich said.

"No time to find out, sadly." Dad led the way out of the courtyard and into the street beyond. From behind them came the sound of splintering wood as the woman's tirade increased in volume and intensity.

Two streets farther on, they slowed to a walk. All three of them were out of breath and feeling the heat.

"Still bored?" Dad asked Jade.

"Still wanting to have a talk about what happened in Mont Passat," she shot back.

"Ah, that."

"Yes," Rich agreed. "That."

Dad shrugged. "No big deal."

"Being chased through Venice by the Mafia and an Eastern European gangster is no big deal?" said Jade. "You still have some serious lifestyle problems, you know that?"

"I know I could do with a drink," Chance said.

Jade's eyes widened, but Rich had seen Dad's mouth twitch with amusement. "He's teasing you, Jade."

"Well, we can't go back to the hotel. What did Ralph want?" Dad asked before Jade could come back at him.

"Ask him yourself," said Jade.

Rich thought at first she was sulking. Then he saw that a figure had stepped out of a side street just ahead of them. Ralph. Behind them, dark-suited men stepped out of alleyways and alcoves and stood with arms folded—blocking any hope of another escape.

5

Jade's fists were clenched so tight her nails dug into her palms. She was tense, ready to run as soon as Dad gave the word. The Mafia men stayed where they were while Ralph walked confidently toward Jade, Rich and Dad. He had his arms spread and hands open as if to show he meant them no harm.

"As I told Rich," Ralph said, "I want to give you a warning."

"Threats?" Dad sounded amused at the idea.

"No. I think that's what Rich assumed. But no—no threats. A friendly warning. For your own good."

"Go on then," Jade said. "Just warn us, then we can all go."

Ralph was right in front of them now. "First, I must apologize. I didn't mean to worry or frighten or offend you. But as you will soon appreciate, this is important—to you rather than to me. So I am sorry for the slightly . . . extreme measures I have taken."

"You can't say 'slightly extreme,'" Rich told him. "Something's either extreme or it isn't."

Ralph nodded. "Extreme but well intentioned, then. Let me make it up to you." He smiled suddenly, turning in an instant into a genial host. "Let me offer you a late lunch. After all, with all that running you must have worked up quite an appetite. I know I have."

"So, you chase us half across Venice, then offer us a pizza?" Dad said. "You always did do things differently, Ralph. If it is Ralph today. Only I've known you by so many names."

"Hardly unusual in our profession, Mr. Chance. Or is it Mr. Ronson? Or David Melbor? Last time we met, you were Harry . . ." He clapped his hands together. "Anyway, the offer stands. Lunch at my villa—or rather, the villa my local colleagues have put at my disposal. Lunch and a friendly chat and some good vintage wine. Or possibly," he said, looking from Jade to Rich, "good vintage lemonade."

"Oh, well," said Jade, "if there's going to be lemonade."

Ralph's speedboat was large and fast. It cut through the canal, leaving a V in the water and setting gondolas rocking and gondoliers shouting. It was also noisy, but with the spray and the wind in her face, Jade found it refreshing. Her blond hair blew around her, and she pushed it from her eyes.

"Aren't you hot in that jacket?" Rich asked the skull-faced man, who was sitting opposite them in the back of the boat.

His suit had soon dried in the heat of the day, and even

without the mask he looked gaunt and menacing. "But where would I hide my gun?" He opened the jacket to reveal a shoulder holster.

"You could try a career change," Jade suggested.

"Get a nice job in an office," Dad agreed.

The man shrugged. "Then I would have to wear a suit anyway."

Ralph turned from where he was standing at the front of the boat and shouted over the sound of the engine, "Scevola loves his work."

"*Family* business?" Dad wondered.

"Oh yes," the skull-faced man—Scevola—said. "And I love my family too."

The boat turned off the main canal, heading into a narrow, private waterway. At the end, Jade could see an enormous house. It was painted pale yellow, and unlike so many of the buildings she had seen by the water, it was clean and dry and in immaculate condition.

Inside, the building was just as impressive. Heavy crystal chandeliers hung from ornately plastered ceilings, and the carpets were so deep it was like walking on a well-kept lawn. Ralph led them along a wide hallway to an enormous drawing room. French windows gave way to a wide terrace overlooking the water, and Ralph gestured for them to sit.

It was bizarre, but Jade found she was feeling more relaxed on the terrace of Ralph's Mafia-supplied house than she had been all holiday. She sipped at iced mineral water and picked at a pasta salad. Okay—pasta yet again. But she'd let Ralph off, just this once.

With the exception of skull-faced Scevola, the other men had left. Ralph did most of the talking. He explained again about the Banker and how he had access to a large number of criminal bank accounts.

"Now the Tiger, he is a very different sort of man," Ralph said. He poured himself more wine, holding the glass up to admire the quality of the pale straw-colored liquid. "Like the Banker, no one knows who he really is or what his name might be. But the Banker, one gets the impression, has some morals. He never deals with terrorists or gets involved with the businesses he handles. He charges a fair price for his services. Up until now he has been efficient and reliable."

"And now you want your money back," Rich said.

Ralph laughed. "It would be nice. But no, that isn't really an issue. Neither Scevola nor I have very much money involved. Yes, the Banker handles matters for us. Now the Tiger, again, is different."

"So tell us about the Tiger," Dad said. "I've heard the stories, of course. But what's the truth?"

"Always a good question," Ralph conceded. "The Tiger—where to begin? Perhaps if I told you that the most unpleasant, the most violent, the most outrageous stories that you might have heard are the most likely to be true. Or that if you have ever heard anything good or redeeming about the Tiger, then forget it."

"He's a gangster?" Rich asked, glancing quickly at Ralph.

Ralph caught the look and laughed. "Nothing so honest."

"He's an investor," Dad said. "He invests money in criminal activity. Organized crime. Blackmail rackets. People trafficking and slavery. Arms sales and mercenaries. And terrorism. Thought to be British or at least European. He started out as an investor, or so it's said. Came from a business background and applied his knowledge and talent to crime."

"But you said the Banker kept away from all that," Jade reminded them.

"The Tiger is the only exception."

"Why?" Rich asked.

"Because he used the Banker right from the start. Didn't want to dirty his hands, wanted to keep one step removed from the actual business of crime. For this reason, even back then, he kept the Banker at arm's length. Not even the Banker has ever met the Tiger—he deals always through intermediaries. It was later, when the Banker already worked for him, that the Tiger expanded his reach into less pleasant activities."

"*Even* less pleasant," Jade qualified.

Ralph raised his glass to her, conceding the point. "And having worked for the Tiger, the Banker knew that he couldn't step away. He knew what would happen to him if he did. The Tiger is probably the only one of his clients who knew who the Banker really was, from the old days when they were both starting out. It may be because of the Tiger that the Banker finally decided to retire."

"Not an easy job to retire from," Dad pointed out. "Which is why he made the death run."

"The what?" Jade asked.

"Disappeared," Ralph said. "Started a new life. Risky, but if you pull it off, it can be worth it. The death run is the closest some of us get to a retirement plan. But somehow the Tiger found out what the Banker was planning and had him brought to Mont Passat."

"You want to take the story from there, Dad?" Jade raised her eyebrows.

He shrugged. "Not a lot to tell. Okay, so I did a bit of business in Mont Passat. That was why Ardman sent us there. I wasn't going to tell you and spoil our break, but it was fairly clear it was a condition of the holiday that I get the Banker away from Mont Passat."

"So you went into the casino, guns blazing," Rich said.

Dad smiled. "Hardly. I walked him out and put him in a car."

"And the drinking and gambling?" Jade said.

"Part of my cover. Had to do it." He grinned. "It was hell, you know."

"Oh, I know," said Jade sarcastically. "We saw the security footage."

"And that," Ralph said, "is why you are here."

"Oh?" Dad held out his glass for more wine. "I haven't seen them, but the images show nothing. I know that. I made sure of it."

"True," Ralph agreed. "I have examined them very carefully. There is no sign of the Banker, nothing to show how he escaped or who helped him. But . . . " He paused to refill his own glass. "But *you* are there, my friend. That is why I wanted to warn you. The camera footage I have is a copy, an expensive copy. But the original is still with the man who actually owns the casino at Mont Passat."

"Guess who," Dad said. "So those rumors are true as well."

"There are several holding companies and offshore investment banks in between. But yes, behind it all is a hidden Tiger. A Tiger who will also be examining those security pictures. A Tiger who will, sooner or later, recognize *you*."

"A Tiger who, like us, does not believe in coincidence." It was the first time that Scevola had spoken, and his tone was severe. "This is of very little interest to me and my colleagues. As Ralph has told you, we lost relatively little when the Banker went. But you are a friend of Ralph's, and he tells us he owes you a favor."

"And the Tiger," Ralph said, "if the rumors are true, has lost rather more. He entrusted the Banker with almost all his funds. The Banker and the Banker alone has the account numbers and access codes that can release those funds. The Tiger will be desperate to find him, to recover the account numbers and codes before he hands them over."

"His bargaining chips," Chance explained. "That's what he'll be offering in return for the death run—access to the money, and the names and details of the people he worked for. A huge coup for Ardman. But the Banker will hold out for the very best deal he can get."

"As long as he holds out, the Tiger will be after the money." Ralph sipped at his wine. "Even after the money is gone, the Tiger will want to get his hands on the Banker. And," he added significantly, "on anyone who helped him get away."

"Dad," said Rich quietly.

"You look for trouble, don't you?" Jade sighed.

"It's my job," he replied.

Ralph turned so he was face-to-face with John Chance. "*That* is the warning, my friend. If I can find out who helped the Banker to escape, then you can be sure that the Tiger can too. And when he does . . ." Ralph shook his head. "Now, who wants gelato?"

6

It was evening by the time they got back to the hotel.

"You go up to the room and get packed," Dad told Rich and Jade as they reached the small lounge bar. "We leave tomorrow, so we might as well be ready."

"And what are you going to do?" Jade asked. "Just off to smuggle some double agent out of the country?"

Dad forced a laugh. "No. But I am going to call Ardman and give him a piece of my mind."

"And warn him about this Tiger?" Rich asked.

Dad nodded. "I expect he already knows. But yes, I'll pass on Ralph's warning." He pulled out his cell phone.

"You're going to phone him from down here?" Jade asked.

"It's impossible to find a bartender when you want a drink, so I think it's the best place if you don't want to be overheard."

"Meaning you don't want *us* to overhear," Rich said.

"You're welcome to stay and listen." He was already dialing.

"Let's go and pack," Jade said.

Dad gave them a wave as he spoke into the phone. "This is Chance. Can you have Mr. Ardman call me back on this number with maximum encryption . . . Yes, it *is* rather urgent."

The hotel manager arrived and offered Chance a drink while he was waiting for his call. The manager was a stooped, middle-aged man with slicked-back hair that was obviously dyed as well as oiled. He poured a double whiskey and dropped in two ice cubes that Chance didn't want.

The phone rang as Chance took a sip of the whiskey. He held the cell phone up for the manager to see. "Private," he said simply.

The manager nodded. He was about to leave, then as an afterthought put the bottle of whiskey on the table beside Chance.

Chance turned away slightly as he answered the call. "Chance here . . . " He waved his appreciation at the manager's disappearing back. "Yeah, I did say it was urgent. I thought you'd like to know that the Mafia and the Krejikistan underworld, and probably every gangster from here to Australia, know about what happened at Mont Passat." Chance explained about his meeting with Ralph and Scevola.

They talked through the implications of Chance's meeting with Ralph for several minutes. Chance asked: "So, any reason to think the Tiger might be looking for us, apart from what I've been told here?"

"None so far," Ardman answered in measured tones. He sounded cautious rather than angry at the events Chance had described. "It's a possibility. We always knew that."

"You didn't tell *me*."

"You didn't need to know."

"So, what *do* I need to know, if not that a sadistic criminal mastermind is looking for me?"

"He's looking for the Banker, not you," Ardman pointed out. "And the good news is that his ability to find you has been severely curtailed since he can't get at most of his money. Unfortunately," he went on, "neither can we. But that's something for me to worry about."

"Is the Banker not coming up with the goods?"

"The Banker is being most helpful. But it seems that he doesn't actually know the account numbers and pass codes we need to get at the funds. The Treasury is all set to freeze the accounts, and the United Nations has a special committee that can agree to seize the funds on an international basis. And now I have to tell them that we can't find the money."

"But how can that be? The Banker—"

"The Banker has so many cutouts and security measures and fail-safes he makes MI5 look like a cheap apartment with broken locks."

"So how do you get the account details?" Chance asked.

"We're working on that. There is a way. But the Banker wants to be absolutely sure he is completely safe before he tells us. So at the moment I have him secure and looked after. He's starting his new life. We've arranged to make sure he feels comfortable that there's help within reach. But you can believe me—the Tiger isn't going to find him."

"Yes, well, I expect I don't need to know," Chance said. "Come to that, I don't *want* to know. And as you say, meanwhile the money's going nowhere, so there's no rush. Not unless the Tiger—"

Ardman cut him off. "Never mind about the Tiger. I think we've blunted his claws, at least for now. You enjoy the rest of your holiday. You're back tomorrow, is that right?"

"That's right. Then straight down to Cleeveholme for the start of school."

"I had your stuff shipped to the cottage from your London flat," Ardman said. "You'll be quite comfortable there. Do you good to have a break, and the children will appreciate you being nearby. I got the distinct impression they didn't want to go to a boarding school."

"At least with me in the village they can live at the cottage instead of in the school. And if I do need to go away, I reckon I can persuade them to stay for a night or two."

"I'm sure that won't be necessary. Not for a while. You're on extended leave; I won't be calling you back in until I'm sure you're settled and everything is working out."

"Thanks," Chance said. "But what's the catch?"

"You're no use to me if your heart and mind are on other matters. And it'll give you the opportunity to get your breath back after Krejikistan and Mont Passat. Sort out your family life."

Chance raised his eyebrows. "I'd better make a start, then," he said, ending the call before Ardman could change his mind.

· · ·

It didn't take Jade and Rich long to pack their things. Apart from clothes, they'd not brought much—a few books and music players.

They had separate rooms, opposite each other across a narrow corridor. Dad's room was next to Rich's. As they packed their stuff, they left the doors open so they could talk. There were very few guests at the hotel apart from themselves, and the floor they were on only had one other room.

"Looking forward to school?" Rich asked.

"Get real," Jade told him.

"I am. Looking forward to it, I mean."

"Yeah, right. Course you are."

"I am," Rich insisted. He left his backpack leaning against the little wardrobe in his room and went over to join Jade. "Really. I think it'll be good. You and me together, a new start. And living in a village—that sounds neat."

"It sounds boring." Jade sat down on her bed. "A village? What's there to do in a village? So far as I can tell, there's our cottage and the school and that's about it."

"There'll be things going on at school, though," Rich said. "They do that at fancy private schools—lots of clubs and after-school stuff."

Jade grunted. "Fancy. Like we'll fit in."

"I doubt if it's really fancy," Rich said. He sat down beside her on the bed. "People with money. That's not the same thing."

"We're not rich either."

"So? No one will know."

"We will."

"Do we care?" Rich asked her.

Jade smiled at that. "No," she said. "No, we don't. A school's a school and kids are kids and we'll make friends and have a good time. And live at home—you, me and . . ." Her smile turned into a frown. "And Dad."

"He's all right."

"I know." Jade sighed. "But just when I think he's being honest with us and we're getting somewhere, he pulls a stunt like at the casino."

Rich nodded. "Yeah. But you know, I was thinking—that's his job. I mean, if he was, I don't know, a car salesman, we'd be upset because we go on holiday and he tries to sell a car to any bloke he meets who seems interested. If he was a writer, he'd be forever scribbling rubbish in some notebook."

Jade considered this. "I guess we're lucky he's not a taxidermist," she said.

Rich laughed. "If he was, we could tell him to get stuffed."

A car arrived for them the next morning. It was the same black limo that Rich had been bundled into the day before. But now its hood was scratched and dented. One of the headlights was cracked, like the face of Rich's watch.

"Compliments of Ralph," the driver told them. It was one of the men who had chased them. "He apologizes for not coming in person, but he is rather busy. He will meet you at the airport."

"There's no need," Dad told the driver. But the driver did not answer as he helped Jade and Rich put their bags in the enormous trunk.

"What happened to your car?" Rich asked, pointing at the hood.

"Best not mention it," Dad said quietly. "Might be a touchy subject."

The car drove them to a quay where Ralph's speedboat was waiting. Then after a noisy, windswept boat trip another large black car—not dented—drove them to the airport. It pulled up in an area clearly marked as "no waiting."

Ralph was standing inside the terminal building. He handed Dad a pile of tickets. "You are already checked in. Mario will organize your luggage, and I have arranged for you to wait in the luxury lounge until your plane is ready. I have boarding passes for you here. Security is a nightmare these days, you know. I even had to show them your passports."

"You don't have our passports," Rich told him.

"I know," Ralph said. "Like I said—a nightmare. But all sorted out now." He handed the boarding passes to Dad. "Oh, I'm sorry to see Her Majesty's government is clearly cutting back on things, so I took the opportunity to upgrade you to first class. I hope that's all right."

"Nice," Jade told him. "Thanks."

"You're too kind," Dad said. "But don't expect any favors in return."

"As if." Ralph smiled. "Now, I will say goodbye and I wish you good luck. May you enjoy a Tiger-free life."

"I'm sure we will. But thanks for the warning." Dad turned to Rich and Jade. "Come on, then, just time to look in the tacky gift shops before we head for the lounge."

"Ah!" Ralph called them back. "No need—I almost forgot. I have taken care of that too." He pulled a small package wrapped in tissue paper from his jacket pocket.

"You've bought us tacky gifts," Dad said, amused.

"I'm not sure *tacky* is the word I would use. But gifts, yes—to apologize again for the inconvenience."

The package was in fact three small packages. Ralph weighed each in his hand and felt each one carefully before handing them out.

Jade unwrapped hers and found it contained a necklace of large bright blue glass beads.

"Murano glass," Ralph explained. "Handmade. Unique. I, er, had to buy rather a lot of Murano glass yesterday. Some of it broken. A slight accident in a local shop."

Rich had a watch. "Is it real?" he asked, seeing the Rolex name across the dial.

"It is a real watch," Ralph told him with a smile. "But, knowing where it came from, I cannot vouch one hundred percent for its authenticity. But it tells the time, so what more could you want? I noticed you could do with a new one."

"Thanks," Rich said. "It's pretty impressive, real or not." He put on the watch, stuffing his old one with the cracked face into his pocket. The new watch was chunky and heavy.

Ralph helped Jade put on the necklace as Dad unwrapped his gift.

"The beads match your eyes," Ralph told Jade. "Perfect."
She smiled, unable to hide her appreciation.

Dad held up a silver hip flask. "Thank you." He shook it
gently. "And you filled it for me."

"Mineral water," Ralph said. He smiled at Jade, then
watched with amusement as Dad unscrewed the top and
sniffed at the contents.

Dad moved the flask from his nose quickly and blinked
rapidly.

"Special Russian mineral water," Ralph explained. "The
flask, I am told, could stop a bullet. Which seemed appropri-
ate. After all—you never know."

"Maybe not," Dad said. "But I doubt it'll be necessary. I
spoke to Ardman last night, passed on your message."

"Good. And?"

"And we are both agreed," Dad said. "There's really no
way the Tiger can find the Banker or me. Thanks for the concern—and for the gifts and the upgrade—but we'll be quite
safe."

7

The Tiger had been summoned to a meeting. He did not like being summoned, but sometimes it was important to maintain a facade, to do things he didn't like.

His cell phone phone rang as he approached the conference room. He glanced at the caller name, then excused himself. "I think I'd better take this," he told the people with him, putting down his expensive leather briefcase.

Bannock's voice was loud and excited in his ear. "We've got something!"

"About time too, if I may say so," the Tiger said quietly. He turned slightly to smile and wave at his colleagues, gesturing for them to go ahead into the conference room.

"On the CCTV and from talking to the staff at the casino."

"You've found how he got out?"

"No. But we have identified a suspect. Someone I think you'll be interested in. Someone who was at the casino that night and left the next morning."

"That sounds very promising. Do we know where this person is now?"

"Working on it," Bannock said. "He went from Mont Passat to Venice. We're checking departures now. Should have an answer soon."

"The sooner the better," the Tiger told him. "This is very important to me, Bannock. *Very* important." He didn't need to spell out the consequences of failure.

"I understand. I'll call you again as soon as I have more news."

"I'll look forward to it." For the first time in days, the Tiger was feeling good. Things were coming together at last. He pushed his phone into his jacket pocket, picked up his briefcase and walked briskly to the conference room.

It looked as though everyone else was there. The man who had called the meeting was standing at the head of the table, ready to start.

"I'm sorry to keep you waiting," the Tiger said, making his way to his seat. As he passed the man standing at the head of the table, he added: "I do hope this won't take long, Mr. Ardman."

8

Jade wouldn't admit it, but she actually enjoyed the twenty-minute walk every morning from Dad's cottage to the school—though she knew that might change as the autumn weather kicked in. The first ten minutes were the best—through the all-but-deserted village. The second half of the walk was along the winding school driveway, up a shallow incline and through a wooded area. Finally, the old manor house appeared as they turned a bend in the drive. The old house had been added to when it became a school. There was a new block with the school auditorium, math and English classrooms and an adjoining computer lab. The newer parts of the building dwarfed the Georgian splendor of the main house.

It was a lovely walk. But by this time, other children were arriving. Rich and Jade were the only pupils from the tiny village, but some children came on a local bus that stopped at the bottom of the drive. Because the one-way system in and out of the school meant there were always lines of traffic, a lot more children were dropped at the gates and walked up the drive—with Jade and Rich.

Not that they were bad kids. Jade found she got on better than she expected with most of them. She'd even made a few hesitant friends in her class over the past few weeks. It was the teachers who were a pain—who told Jade she had an "attitude" and who always thought they knew best. If she was quiet in class, they told her off for being uncommunicative. If she made an effort and joined in, she was showing off.

Rich, on the other hand, fit in fine. He'd joined a computer gaming group and the drama club and had already got a couple of good grades. No one had said it yet, but Jade knew from experience that it was only a matter of time: "Why can't you be more like your brother?"

It was a shock to her when she realized that this was something her father had never said.

"We said we'd give it a semester," Rich reminded Jade as they joined the stream of pupils heading up the drive. "Dad agreed. At least, he didn't say no."

"We're here for good," Jade said glumly. "Though I guess it's no worse than anywhere else."

"You kidding? The cottage is great. Better than the small flat in London with just one bedroom between us."

"And the bullet-holed wallpaper. Yeah." Jade paused to glare at Mike Alten from their class, who'd caught her words and was staring at her. He laughed nervously, obviously thinking she was joking. His laugh stopped as it occurred to him that maybe she wasn't.

"It's quiet and out of the way and exclusive," Rich was saying. "Just what Dad and Ardman want."

"Doesn't matter what they want," Jade told him. "What do *we* want?"

"I'm happy enough." He grinned and swung slightly so he nudged her with his backpack. "And you don't know what you want, do you?"

"I want to be able to bring my cell phone into school," Jade said.

"Against the rules. No phones. Not even for the boarders."

They were walking past the block where the boarders lived. It was a modern block separate from the rest of the school buildings. About thirty children lived at the school. At the end of the school day, the boarders were sent back there to do their homework and get their tea. Then they could watch TV and generally fool around until their bedtimes.

"I know what I *don't* want," Jade muttered. "I don't want to spend the evening stuck in detention while you're at drama."

Rich laughed. "Should have thought about that in geography instead of drawing a cartoon of Miss Fletcher. With a mustache and horns."

The teachers took turns running detention. Whichever teacher was in charge decided where it would be—usually in their own classroom so they could get on with some preparation or grading papers. Jade had been in detention a few days before, when it was run by Mr. Rawlings, the PE instructor. He'd made them take desks out onto the all-weather sports field and sit there in the cold drizzle for two hours. Jade had told him exactly what she thought of it.

Which was why she was back tonight. And despite having promised Dad that she would do her best to avoid getting any more detentions, she was already booked for tomorrow as well. But at least this time they were indoors. The new math teacher, Mr. Argent, was taking his turn tonight and tomorrow, so they were upstairs in the main math room.

As she was the only one, Jade concentrated on her work and the time went quickly. When it was over, Jade gathered her things and stuffed them in her backpack.

"I'm off now, okay?" she said.

Mr. Argent was a small man, new to the school, with thinning gray hair and little round glasses that were so thick they made his eyes look enormous through them. He glanced up from his grading and nodded.

"I'll see you tomorrow, then, Jade." He had a slight accent—French, Jade guessed.

"Good night," she muttered as she left. Dad had said he'd walk up to meet them. Which probably meant another lecture on not getting into detention.

Dad and Rich were waiting for her in the main reception area downstairs, outside the auditorium. Rich had been at computer club and was talking excitedly to Dad about it.

"Glad someone's enjoyed himself," said Jade. She slumped down on one of the chairs for visitors.

"You'd enjoy things more if you didn't get into so much trouble," Dad told her.

Jade tightened her lips. "I do enjoy being here," she said. "There are places I'd rather be, but I've been in worse dumps. It's okay."

"Height of praise," Dad said.

"And I do try. I want to learn. They just don't realize it."

"Maybe you don't make it easy for them to realize it." Dad held up his hands before she could reply. "We'll talk about it later, all right? But I know what you mean, okay? It's difficult fitting in and settling down, and if you don't feel you're being appreciated, that makes it even harder. I'm not going to tell you off or get upset. Let's talk about how to make it work. Let me tell you something," he went on in a low voice, "something that the teachers and staff here probably don't realize themselves."

"What's that?" Jade folded her arms, but she was intrigued. Rich stepped closer as he listened too.

"You don't work for them. You don't do lessons and homework and everything else for their benefit. It took me a long time to figure that out when I was at school, then one day it occurred to me."

"What do you mean?" Jade asked.

"*They* work for *you*. All these people, they're here to help you. We pay them. Well, actually, Ardman pays them right now, but it's the same at every school, whether it's fees or taxes or whatever. We pay these people to think of ways to help you learn, to look at your work and tell you how you can improve. To get you through exams that will equip you for whatever you want to do when you're older. But—and it's a big but—they need your help too." He stood up and offered a hand to Jade.

"Thanks." She let him pull her up from the chair.

"Lecture over. But think about it. Right, time we were on our way." He turned to go and suddenly froze.

"What is it?" Jade asked.

Dad was looking past her, back down the main corridor. His face was etched with concern.

Rich laughed. "It's just Mr. Argent."

The little math teacher had finished his marking and was walking slowly toward reception.

"That's Mr. Argent?" Dad said, still staring.

"Yeah," said Jade. "Is that a problem?"

Dad shook his head. "No. No problem at all." He shrugged. "Just doesn't look much like a math teacher, that's all."

"What do math teachers usually look like?" asked Rich.

"I don't know. He isn't what I expected. It's no big deal."

"I think he's French," Jade said. "Maybe French math teachers look different."

Mr. Argent looked from Jade and Rich to their father. He opened his mouth to say something, but Dad got in first.

"Good to meet you, Mr. Argent. I hear you're new. I'm Jade and Rich's dad, but maybe you knew that?"

They shook hands. "No, I didn't know that," Argent said. "But now that you mention it, I can tell."

"So, how are they doing?" Dad asked.

Mr. Argent nodded, looking from Rich to Jade. "Very well,

I think. They both have ability. Rich is very applied. A little steady and safe in his work, perhaps."

"And Jade?" Dad asked. She folded her arms, waiting for the criticism and the could-try-harder.

"Volatile," Mr. Argent said. "Obviously, we're only a few weeks into term, but I think with a bit of commitment and interest, she'll do very well. When she pays attention and decides she wants to work at it, she has flashes of brilliance, if that's not too strong a word." He smiled, and the light caught his glasses as he leaned forward. "Yes, slow and steady might win the race, but it can be a little boring. You know, Rich could learn a lot from his sister."

Jade's mouth dropped open.

Dad seemed pensive and quiet on the walk home. He'd asked to have a few words with Mr. Argent in private and sent Rich and Jade on ahead. As they made their way down the drive, Rich wondered if Dad was thinking about how to get Jade interested in school.

"Do you think Mr. Argent is right?" he asked.

"What about?" asked Jade.

"About you," Rich said.

"Course he's right—I'm brilliant. You can learn a lot from me. Is that a problem?"

Rich shook his head.

"It doesn't matter if he's right," Dad said, catching up with them up. "Though I expect he is."

"How do you mean?" Jade asked.

"Just by saying what he did, he's got you interested, hasn't he? Might be a self-fulfilling prophecy."

"I like math," Jade said. "Math is good."

"I didn't really think much of Mr. Argent as a teacher," Rich said.

"Maybe not," Dad told him. "But he understands people. Oh, and for your information, Jade, he isn't French. He's Swiss. Now, tomorrow I have to go to London."

"What for?" Jade asked.

"I need to see Ardman about something. He's not expecting me, so I might have to wait around. I could be quite late getting back. Will you be okay?"

"We'll be fine," Jade said. "Just so long as you're not getting involved in anything dodgy."

"Yes, well, that's why I want to see Ardman—to make sure I'm not."

"That's okay," Rich said. "We're both busy after school tomorrow."

"Really? What are you up to?"

"Drama club," Rich told him. "I went last week. It was pretty good. Didn't finish till late, remember?"

They were almost at the cottage now. "Good to see you getting into things a bit too, Jade," Dad said. "These after-school activities are important. It's good to get involved."

Rich coughed. "Nearly home," he said. Jade said nothing.

"So what is it you're signed up for after school tomorrow?" Dad asked.

"More detention," said Jade.

9

Drama club ran after school in the auditorium. Detention was at the same time, and Jade had agreed to meet Rich in school reception as soon as they were both free so they could walk back home together. Tonight there were three of them in detention—Jade, Mike Alten and a boy called Rupam from the year below.

Once in the sixth form you didn't get detention, Jade had learned. You were put on "jankers," which meant you got an evening clearing out a ditch or cutting the grass or repainting the corridor. It sounded like a lot more fun than the math exercises Mr. Argent had given her, but she knew better than to complain—she'd learned that, at least.

"Has your wallpaper really got bullet holes in it?" Mike Alten asked Jade quietly as they chose their places in the big classroom.

"Better believe it," Jade said.

"Wicked. Designer stuff, I suppose."

Jade didn't answer.

Mr. Argent was talking quietly and urgently into his phone. He ended the call, placed his phone carefully on the desk beside a pile of exercise books and clapped his hands together for quiet. "Right, we'll have silence now, please." He sat down at his desk and started on the pile of exercise books, pausing only to tell Rupam not to tap his pen on the table.

Rich was enjoying himself. There were only eight students doing drama this week, all from Rich's year and below as the sixth form had their own separate drama group. Most of them were girls—including Gemma Stroud, who was in the same set of classes as Rich for most things. They got along well, and it was good to have someone there that he knew.

Miss Whitfield ran the group. She was young and enthusiastic and had started by getting them all to pretend to be clowns and mime putting on makeup in front of an imaginary mirror. Now a boy from the year below was pretending to be a zookeeper washing a large elephant inside a small cage. The rest of them watched from the front of the stage as he performed in the main area of the auditorium—which seemed a bit backward to Rich. But with all the chairs put away, there was a lot more space.

At the back of the auditorium there was a gallery, like a wide balcony right across the width of the room. The teachers sat up there for school assemblies, and there was a door at the back that led into a storeroom at the end of the math corridor.

A long, low rumble of thunder came from outside. It was getting dark, Rich saw. Along both sides of the auditorium long windows reached almost to the ground. It was cloudy outside, and he could definitely hear thunder. Summer was over, and autumn was rolling in.

"Right, now we're going to split up into pairs and take it in turns to wash elephants," Miss Whitfield said.

"Gemma?" Rich asked at once.

"Why not? Got your elephant?"

"Never go anywhere without it," Rich told her. "I keep it in my trunk."

"Oh, ho ho." Gemma laughed sarcastically.

They jumped off the stage. The thunder was louder now. It sounded very close.

"Storm coming," Gemma said as the sound rumbled on.

Everyone had spread out in the auditorium, leaving him and Gemma closest to the stage, opposite the emergency exit. Rich looked out through the glass of the doors again as the sound got even closer. There was another sound mixed in with it too. It was like gunfire. He smiled to himself—what a stupid idea.

There was someone running—heading straight for the doors. Silhouetted against the darkening sky outside. A woman. She was almost at the doors, but she showed no sign of slowing down.

"Look out!" Gemma shouted, seeing her too.

It did no good. The woman hit the double doors at full

speed, bursting them open. One door flew right around and hit the wall behind so hard the glass shattered. Everyone turned to look.

The woman crashed to the floor, one hand stretched out—clenched in a fist. But Rich barely noticed. He was staring at her face where it was turned against the floor, at the long auburn hair spread out over her back.

The back of the pale gray coat she was wearing was spattered with blood.

"She's been shot!" Rich exclaimed.

The woman's fingers relaxed and opened. Something dropped from them, falling and rolling across the floor. It bounced toward Rich, its facets catching the light like glass.

Nothing else would be shaped like that.

Nothing else would sparkle like that.

It could only be a huge diamond.

"Oh, good God!" Miss Whitfield shrieked. "Careful now, everyone. Let me see if I can get some help. First aid."

"Who *is* she?" someone else asked.

Miss Whitfield shifted from one foot to the other. "I shall have to phone for an ambulance from the school office. This is terrible . . . how did this . . ." Panic seeped into the teacher's voice.

"Maybe she's got a cell phone," Rich said. "We can call for help." He knelt beside the woman. The sight of the blood made him feel light-headed and faint, but he was relieved to see she was still breathing. Rich reached a trembling hand into the pocket of her coat. There was no phone, at least not in that pocket. But he pulled out something else—something sharp and hard. A handful of much smaller diamonds that glittered and shone.

"What's going on?" Rich wondered out loud.

He was aware of Gemma beside him holding the large diamond—the size and shape of a half lemon. Miss Whitfield leaned over, her face white. The other children clustered behind her—not wanting to see, but unable to look away.

Rich's mind was racing as he stood up. He took the diamond from Gemma and turned it over in his hand. "If she's been shot, that *was* gunfire. Which means someone must—"

But he didn't get any further. At that moment, all around the room, the windows exploded into sharp flying fragments of glass. Figures in black combat clothes leaped and crashed into the auditorium, machine guns ready and aimed right at Rich and the others.

10

The sound of breaking glass was loud even up in the math room. Jade jumped to her feet.

"What was that?" Mr. Argent said.

"Someone dropped something," Mike suggested.

"People doing drama, in the auditorium," Rupam said. "They were playing with toy guns just now. I heard them."

"That was thunder," said Mike.

"I'll go and see," Jade decided.

"I really don't think that's necessary," Mr. Argent told her.

Ignoring Mr. Argent, Jade hurried from the room and ran down the math corridor. There were several other rooms along the way and a narrow flight of stairs down to the school's main reception area. But the corridor ended in a smaller room that was used for storage.

Jade made her way past piles of textbooks to the door at the back of the room. She opened it carefully, some instinct warning her to be as quiet as possible. The door led to the gallery at the back of the auditorium. Jade could hear noises from below—a man speaking, Miss Whitfield's nervous replies, someone crying . . . What was going on?

As she approached the front of the gallery, Jade could gradually see more and more of the auditorium below. She held her breath and slowed to a hesitant tiptoe. Her heart thumped, and Jade felt herself go cold with dread as she saw the men with guns, the woman with her distinctive auburn hair sprawled on the floor and the group of frightened children with Miss Whitfield.

And finally—thankfully—Rich. He was standing slightly apart from everyone else, closer to the stage, with Gemma Stroud. Somehow Jade had to get him out of there. She didn't know what was going on, but if it didn't have something to do with their dad, then she'd be very surprised.

A tall, broad-shouldered hulk of a man seemed to be in charge. He had a fierce red beard. He was gesturing for Miss Whitfield and the children to move away from the unconscious—or dead?—woman. His men herded them back toward the stage, making them sit along the front with their hands on their knees.

"You all do as you're told, and no one need get hurt." He was a big man with a Scottish accent. "Just sit there, good as gold, while we get what we came for. I'll probably have some questions for you in a minute. And don't get any ideas about calling for help. We've got this place locked down. No phones in or out. Cell phones are jammed too. There are police at the gates to tell any of your parents who might turn up for you to wait a bit and not to worry. Same goes for the dorm up the drive. So far as they know, there's a dangerous criminal got into the school and everyone's to stay put till the police sort it out." He grinned suddenly, teeth appearing in the middle of the red beard. "And what do you know—there *is* a dangerous criminal loose in the school. A whole lot of them, in fact."

Several of the gunmen laughed as the bearded man guffawed at his own joke. Jade moved slowly back toward the door to the storeroom. If Rich had any hope of getting away, she needed to create a diversion. A diversion that didn't involve getting shot.

Jade found what she wanted just inside the storeroom—a particularly heavy textbook. She eased back toward the front of the gallery. Fortunately all the gunmen were watching their leader and the captives sitting along the front of the stage. Jade risked a wave, trying to attract Rich's attention. But of course he was watching the gunmen.

As she got more desperate, Jade was afraid she would not get anyone's attention. But eventually, Gemma noticed her. Even from the other end of the auditorium, Jade saw her tense slightly. Gemma nudged Rich, and he followed the direction of her stare. As he saw Jade, he smiled. He gave the smallest nod.

The next problem was how to tell Rich what she was going to do. Jade held up the book and Rich frowned. Did he think she was wanting help with her math detention? She brandished the book like it was her dearest possession. Then she mimed throwing it. Again Rich nodded—so far, so good. But even with a distraction, what could he do?

Rich glanced around, still assessing his rather limited options for when Jade threw the book. If the gunmen were looking for the big diamond, he would prefer they didn't find it in his pocket. Should he chuck it away? The best thing would be to escape himself. But how?

They'd started the first drama session last week with a tour of the little backstage area of the auditorium. Miss Whitfield had pointed out the wheel you turned to open and close the curtains, the way the backdrops could be slotted in and out, the lighting controls in a booth at the front of the auditorium and something else too that Rich thought might be useful. If only he had time.

He nudged Gemma. "Stay here," he whispered. "Look after everyone. You'll be safest if you stay put and do as they tell you."

She stared at him, eyes wide.

On the gallery at the far end of the auditorium, Jade was holding up three fingers. She'd count to three. She held the book up in one hand—ready. With the other hand she showed thumbs-up. Then finger and thumb: two. Thumb and two fingers: three.

She threw the book, tossing it just far enough for it to arc over the end of the gallery. Already Jade was backing away, ready to escape.

The book landed with a loud *thwack*. The gunmen all

turned toward the sound. Rich scrambled back across the stage, Gemma shifting along slightly to disguise the gap where he had been.

"Come on, come on," he breathed urgently to himself, scrabbling at the small metal ring in the stage floor. The trap-door was heavy, but he managed to swing it open and dropped into the space below, lowering the door quickly behind him. He held it slightly open, making sure there was no sound as he gently closed it.

Rich crouched in the darkness. He could hear shouting from the auditorium, people moving. Then gunfire. He hardly dared to breathe, knowing that if he moved at all, he might knock into something. And he realized that he had no idea how to get out from beneath the stage.

Jade heard the book land, saw Rich moving quickly to a trap-door—good idea! Almost immediately, there were shouts from below. The red-bearded man was turning full circle, gun raised as he looked for where the book had come from.

She was almost back at the storeroom when he caught sight of her. The man's gun came up. Fire spat from the end of it and Jade hurled herself backward. She tripped on the step up to the door and fell heavily. A line of bullet holes erupted from the door frame level with where her head had been. She scrambled backward and pulled the door shut.

But not before she heard the bearded man shouting at several of his gunmen to get up to the gallery. Did they know the way to the math corridor? Didn't matter, Jade realized as she heard the sounds from below—they were climbing up the sup-porting pillars under the gallery. Coming after her.

She dashed through the storeroom, pulling piles of books over behind her—anything to slow them down. As she emerged into the corridor outside, she slammed into a figure standing in the doorway and gave a cry of surprise and fear.

"What on earth's going on?" Mr. Argent asked. "That was gunfire!"

"Oh, thank God it's you," Jade gasped.

"What's happening?"

"Men with guns. Right behind me. Come on!" She grabbed his arm.

Judging from the sounds coming from the storeroom—more books and furniture being pushed aside—she figured there wasn't time to get back to Mr. Argent's room. Jade led the way quickly to the narrow stairs.

"What about those other boys?" Mr. Argent asked quietly.

"Mike and Rupam? Have to hope we lead the gunmen away."

"What a thing to have to hope for," he said grimly.

The darkness seemed to diminish slightly as Rich's eyes grew used to it. He could make out shapes, darker patches where there were support struts for the stage above. Soon he was confident enough to start crawling through the space, head-ing for the back of the stage and hoping there was a way out. Miss Whitfield hadn't told them how you got out from the trapdoor . . .

The sounds from the auditorium were muffled. But he could make out the shouts of one of the gunmen.

"Barney's gone after them, down the stairs. These two were hiding in a classroom up there. They said they were in detention."

"Find a way back down here and bring them with you," the Scotsman replied—louder and closer. "Let's keep them all together in here."

There was silence for a while, and Rich found himself at the back wall of the stage. He felt carefully along the back and the underside, trying to find a way out—an opening or another trapdoor. But there was nothing. Dust was beginning to clog his throat and nostrils, and he was terribly afraid he would have to cough.

"Right," the leader shouted. "Pearson, you and Gray stay in here with the kids and anyone else we come across. The rest of us, let's find what we came for and get out of here."

Someone said something else, but Rich couldn't hear their words, just a muffled rumble of sound.

"Ah, she's out of it," the Scotsman replied. "Maybe she'll bleed to death, though the wound's not too bad. When I aim to shoot someone in the shoulder, I damn well shoot them in the shoulder. But if we get what we came for, we won't need her anyway. She was useful to lead us here."

Rich had crawled all the way to the side of the stage now. He had his hand pressed against the underside as he went. Right at the edge, in the corner, he suddenly felt the boards above him give slightly. Trying not to get his hopes up, he pushed hard and felt the stage above him move. Another trap-door—but where did it come out? If it was in full view of the gunmen in the auditorium, he was in serious trouble.

A strip of dim light shone in through the widening gap as he pushed the door slowly upward. Was it Rich's imagination, or was the light not as bright as he would have expected? After so much time under the stage in near darkness, it was difficult to tell.

As soon as the opening was big enough, Rich peered out. It *was* darker here because it was in shadow. He was in the wings—off to the side of the stage and out of sight from the auditorium.

Rich climbed out. There was a fire door at the side of the stage, with a long metal bar across it you pushed to unlatch it. Miss Whitfield had mentioned that during a performance, they kept the door open so the actors could get in and out to the classrooms they used for costume changing and makeup.

Opening the door was bound to make some noise. Rich took a deep breath, preparing to run, and pressed the opening bar. The door opened so easily it took Rich by surprise.

But not as much as the immediate loud ringing of the fire alarm.

A few minutes earlier, Jade had been running. But she didn't think Mr. Argent could outrun the gunman clattering down the stairs close behind them. So as they ran, she pulled off her school tie.

The bottom of the narrow staircase emerged in a corridor

just off the main reception foyer outside the auditorium. As the walls stopped, metal banisters replaced them.

As soon as they reached the bottom of the stairs, Jade bent down and looped her tie through one of the rails, quickly knotting it about fifteen centimeters up the metal strut. "Keep going," she hissed at Mr. Argent. "I'll catch up with you."

"But what—"

"Just go!"

Jade doubled back into the space beside the staircase, pulling the tie across the width of the step. If the gunman was watching where he was going, he'd see the tie and he'd see Jade.

So when the alarm bell started just as the gunman rounded the last corner of the stairs, Jade almost whooped for joy.

He looked up, searching for the source of the sound—and failing to see the tie stretched across the stairs. He was still running fast, desperate to catch his prey.

His foot caught so hard on the tie that it was wrenched from Jade's hands. Her palms burned from the friction.

But the gunman came off worse. He was propelled headlong from several steps up, his cry of surprise lost in the sound of the bell. There was a sickening crunch as the man crashed down. His chin bounced off the floor and blood sprayed from his nose. His gun slid away from him, but he made no move to retrieve it. No move at all.

Jade stood up. The bell died away and there was a moment's silence. Then Mr. Argent appeared from farther down

76

the corridor. He stared in disbelief at the body lying across the corridor and the splatters of blood.

"Let's see if we can lock him up somewhere before he comes around," Jade said.

"What happened?"

Jade stuffed her tie into her blazer pocket. "He fell for it."

It was a relief when the alarm stopped. Rich cursed himself for not realizing the fire door was linked to the alarm system. But the gunmen had presumably disabled it by now. At least they didn't know what had set it off. They might guess it was a door, but they didn't know which one.

Rich ran quickly down the hall. He wanted to find Jade. From what the chief gunman had said, it didn't sound like there was any hope of phoning for help. And if there were fake police and other gunmen out in the grounds, then escape might be difficult too. But if he could find Jade, then together they could discover what the intruders were after . . .

The door into the main reception outside the auditorium was made of safety glass, so Rich could see into the foyer. With the lights on inside, he hoped that no one in the area would be able to see him watching from outside. Because the bearded chief of the gunmen and another of the intruders were standing by the reception desk. They were looking at something beside it, on the wall. What was it? A picture?

It was difficult to remember what was on that wall. There were class photos and framed news clippings, sports certificates and achievement awards all around the reception area. There was even a large glass cabinet full of sports trophies and medals. But that was on the other side of the foyer. Rich went as close to the door as he dared—any closer and surely they would see him.

As he watched, the bearded man tapped on the wall—on the glass over a large picture, Rich could see now. Then the man raised the gun that was strapped over his shoulder. He turned it in a single, swift movement and smashed the butt into the glass. Then he reached in through the hole he had made and took something out—something small and square.

With a grin of satisfaction, the man showed it to his colleague and they both marched quickly away.

Rich counted to twenty after they had gone, then let himself into the foyer. He could see at once what had been so interesting to the gunmen. It was a board showing photographs of all the school staff. The glass over the board was in pieces now, and there was an empty space where just one picture had been removed.

The printed name tag under the photograph was still there. It told Rich what—or rather who—the gunmen had come for.

MR. D. J. ARGENT—MATH & ECONOMICS

11

It was not until almost seven o'clock that John Chance got to see Ardman. When he did, the man was unrepentant and unsympathetic.

"We had to put him somewhere," he told Chance.

"At the same school as my children?" Chance was furious. He paced up and down in front of Ardman's desk as he spoke.

Ardman sighed. "You will recall that we agreed for Rich and Jade to go to Cleeveholme Manor because it is out of the way, not well known, quiet and safe. Where better, you said, for them to lose themselves?"

"I remember," Chance replied.

"Well, the same holds true in this case, surely. I've used the school as a safe house, a staging point for people of all ages in the past. Not that they realize that, of course. You surely cannot assume that you and your children have an exclusive right to safety and anonymity? A safe haven that not even my own superiors know anything about?" He shook his head sadly. "Never had you down as a hypocrite, John."

"I'm not. This is different."

"Oh? We need somewhere to hide our new friend the Banker while we make certain arrangements and he organizes some information we need. Where better than a remote, little-known private school where he can impart some of his undoubted knowledge and experience to children eager to learn from him? Including your own children." Ardman smiled. "I'm doing them a favor, when you think about it."

"You are doing nothing of the sort," Chance retorted angrily. "You've sent them somewhere you said was safe, only you forgot to mention you're also hiding a man there that half the world's gangsters are looking for. Including the Tiger."

Ardman shrugged. "But they aren't going to find him."

"Can you be sure of that?"

"You know as well as I do that in our business, one cannot be sure of anything. So we have to plan for any and every eventuality."

Chance considered this. "You mean, you have a contingency plan? Some way that the Banker can call for help and backup if he needs it?"

"Of course," Ardman assured him.

"Well, that's something, I suppose." Chance was calming a little. Maybe having protection nearby wasn't a bad thing. Especially if there was anything in Ralph's anxieties. "So, who is it?" he asked. "You got Goddard down there staying in a bed-and-breakfast? Or Kyle, maybe . . ."

"Not exactly." Ardman shifted slightly in his chair.

Chance leaned across Ardman's desk. "It's me, isn't it?" He could see from Ardman's expression that he was right. "When were you going to tell me?"

"I was hoping not to have to," Ardman admitted. "But since you ask . . . Yes, the Banker knows there is someone in the village on call if he needs them. He doesn't know it is you, of course."

"He does now," Chance said. "It won't have taken him long to work it out. How does he make contact?"

"He has the number of your cell phone. His own phone is linked direct to a satellite—one of our Mercury series, so it's unjammable and fully encrypted. Any trouble, he can call you."

"It's that simple."

"I like simple. Simple works. People remember simple. There is one other thing."

"And what's that?"

"If he does call, get to him as fast as you can. We need him, John. And if he calls, you'll know all hell's breaking loose."

It was getting darker as the evening drew in, but Rich didn't dare put the lights on. He crept across the school office to the school secretary's desk. She kept it clear and tidy. Just in and out trays, a pile of large notebooks and ledgers, and the phone. A light blinked on the phone, showing there was a message. Not that Rich cared. He wasn't here to pick up messages but to send them.

He glanced around, keenly aware that anyone out in the foyer could look in through the glass hatchway where visitors signed in and see him. But there was no one. Rich lifted the phone and reached out to dial.

Silence. There was no dial tone. He frowned and tried putting the phone back, then lifting it again. But there was still nothing. Maybe you needed to press nine for an outside line or something. That didn't do anything either—none of the numbers did. And Rich went cold as he remembered the bearded gunman saying they'd cut off the phones. He wasn't kidding. Rich could see now that the flashing light on the phone was labeled **LINE**. It was telling him there was no connection.

With Mr. Argent's help, Jade dragged the unconscious gunman to a small store cupboard where the caretaker kept cleaning equipment. They bundled him inside, then went back for his gun.

"I suppose you know how to use that?" Mr. Argent asked as Jade picked it up.

"Well, point it and pull the trigger, I guess. But not really. You?" she asked.

He shook his head.

"Not much use to us, then, is it?" Jade said. "We'll find somewhere to dump it. And we need somewhere to hide while we work out what to do."

"The staff room is along here," Mr. Argent pointed out.

"Good idea. It'll be comfy. And there are several doors in and out, so we won't be trapped. I hope."

The staff room was furnished with a sofa and several easy chairs—all of which had been better days. Jade stuffed the machine gun under the sofa. The room was almost completely dark, but Jade didn't want to risk putting on the lights.

"Now what?" Mr. Argent asked. He perched nervously on one of the small armchairs, rubbing his hands together.

"Good question. It would help if we knew what these people were after."

"Ah." Mr. Argent looked away guiltily. When he looked back at Jade, he seemed even more pale and nervous. "I'm afraid," he said, "that they want *me*."

12

Jade stared at him. "You? Why would they want you? I mean, I assumed it was something to do with Dad and maybe . . ." She fell silent as her brain clicked up a gear. There were lots of thoughts and ideas whizzing around in her head, but now they seemed to be dropping into place. "Why did you say you supposed I knew how to use that gun?"

Mr. Argent shrugged. "I just thought you might. Knowing that your father . . ."

"Yes, my father." Jade walked over to him and looked down at the little man, her hands on her hips as their eyes met. "Dad knew you, didn't he? He told me you're from Switzerland—how did he know that? And you knew him and what he does. You're the Banker."

His eyes widened behind the thick lenses of his spectacles. "You know?"

"I do now." Jade rubbed her forehead. She felt like her brain was going to overload. "But what are you doing here? No, no, no," she went on before he could answer. "You're in hiding, aren't you? Dad thought you'd be safe here, just like we're safe here."

"Don't blame your father," the Banker said quietly. "He knew nothing about it until last night. He got me away from Mont Passat—he saved my life, you know."

"Yeah, well, remember that when you grade my next math test," Jade retorted.

"I didn't think I'd have to call on his help again so soon." The Banker stood up, frowning. He was patting his pockets.

"What are you looking for?" Jade asked.

"My phone."

"Won't work," Jade told him. "The guy in charge said they'd jammed all the signals."

"*My* phone will work," the Banker said. "It's linked to a special satellite. And it has a panic feature. All I need to do is press the right sequence and ask for help."

"So where's . . ." Jade remembered the call the Banker had taken earlier, up in the math corridor. "You put it on your desk. In your classroom. After that call. I bet it's still there."

The Banker seemed to shrink in the chair. "After Eleri called. That must be how they found me—they were watching her." In the near darkness, his face had taken on a haunted expression. "If only I knew where she was."

"Eleri? Is she . . . a friend?"

"A colleague. We work together. She has been watching out for me in case Ardman and his people tried to double-cross me. She was watching out for me in Mont Passat when I took the death run."

"This Eleri," said Jade slowly, with a sudden, horrible realization, "is she tall and slim? Figure to die for and long sort of auburn hair?"

The Banker nodded. "You have seen her? You know where she is?"

Jade wasn't sure what to say, how to tell him. She knelt down in front of his chair and took hold of his hands, surprised at how cold they felt. "She's in the auditorium. But . . ."

"But what?"

"I think she's been shot."

The Banker snatched his hands away and turned, looking into the dim recesses of the room. Jade could hear him struggling to control his breathing. A single sob escaped, and he wiped his eyes.

"I'm sorry," Jade said. "I guess she's a friend as well as a colleague, right?"

His voice was so quiet Jade could barely hear him. "Eleri is my daughter," he said. "I must go to her." The Banker stood up and started for the door.

Jade quickly grabbed him. "That'll do no good. You'll never get there."

"I have to try!"

They both froze at the sound of footsteps from outside.

On the other side of the room, the door burst open. Standing silhouetted against the harsh light from the corridor was a man holding a machine gun.

13

Jade froze. But nothing else moved either—the Banker was still, and the gunman in the doorway made no move as well. It took Jade a moment to realize that coming from the brightly lit corridor, he could see nothing in the darkened room.

But then the man stepped inside, feeling for the light switch.

Jade grabbed Mr. Argent's hands and pulled gently, leading him quickly behind the desk.

The lights snapped on. Jade held her breath, finger to her mouth to warn Mr. Argent—or whatever his name really was—to be quiet. Like he needed telling. The man was shaking with fear.

Footsteps—heavy boots on the bare floorboards. The footsteps hesitated, then moved into the room.

Rich had hidden in the shadows under the main stairs up to the math corridor. The gunmen were moving through the school in an orderly manner, checking each room in turn. They were swift and efficient and methodical. But that meant Rich was able to predict exactly where they were headed and keep out of their way.

Eventually, unless he could hide and let them pass without finding him, Rich would be caught—ending up in the last room they got to. Through the window of the school office he had seen the men outside, walking slowly around, watching for anyone who tried to get out. He'd been lucky not to be spotted on his escape from the auditorium.

There was one room that might be safe, he realized. If they were as efficient and clued in as they seemed, they'd have searched there already. If not, then Rich was walking right into danger.

But what choice did he have? He listened carefully for any sound, and, hoping that the silence meant there was no one within sight, he stepped out from under the stairs.

The footsteps moved away again, the lights clicked off and the door slammed shut. Jade and the Banker were safe, at least for the moment.

"I doubt we can get out safely," Jade whispered. "But if we head back to reception, we can get up to the math corridor and back to your classroom."

"And get my phone."

"That's right. How's it work?"

"You need to dial star five five star. That should put you straight through. Just say you need help. They can pinpoint the phone and send someone."

There were still splashes of blood on the floor of the corridor, and Jade wondered if any of the other gunmen had noticed. Was the man she'd tripped up still unconscious? She glanced at the storeroom, half expecting the door to burst open to reveal a furious, bloodstained killer. But it remained closed.

"He'll be out for hours," the Banker said quietly, seeing where Jade had been looking.

They crept up the stairs and emerged into the math corridor close to the little storeroom that led to the gallery above the auditorium.

"So far, so good," Jade murmured. It looked like they were going to get the phone, no problem. And as soon as Ardman sent help . . .

Jade stepped out from the stairs, but the Banker grabbed her shoulder and pulled her back. There was someone in the corridor. A figure walking slowly and purposefully toward them.

"He saw me!" Jade hissed.

"Back down the stairs, then," the Banker said.

Jade couldn't resist a quick glance back down the corridor to see how close the gunman was. Probably running full speed.

But he wasn't. The figure was still walking at the same pace. He waved. Now that he was closer and in the light, Jade could see that it was Rich.

"Surprised to see me?" he asked as he reached them.

He looked rather surprised himself as Jade grabbed him and hugged him tight.

"I'll take that as a yes, then," he said, pulling away at last. "Good to see you too, Jade."

She told him quickly who Mr. Argent really was and about the phone.

"Only problem," Rich said, "is there's one of those guys in the classroom."

"In my classroom?" the Banker said. "A gunman in my classroom?" He sounded more upset about that than he had been about anything else.

"But . . . How do they know it's his classroom?" Jade wondered.

"Says so on the door," Rich told her. "Mr. D. J. Argent."

"They know what I look like, but how do they know that's my new name?" the Banker asked.

"Because they found your photo on the staff mug shot board," Rich explained. "Like, Cleeveholme's most wanted."

"They must have guessed you might go back there. Or they're hoping so," Jade said. "What do we do now?"

"We need to get old Red Beard to call the gunman away," Rich said.

"He's not likely to organize a tea break," Jade pointed out.

"True." Rich grinned. "But if he suddenly needs more men for the search . . ."

Jade was grinning too. "You've got an idea, haven't you?"

"Might have. I reckon they must be getting pretty desperate to find you by now," he said to the Banker. "Let's add to their problems."

14

They hurried into the storeroom and through to the gallery at the back of the auditorium. Looking down, they could see the gunman left on guard and the group of children—now including Mike and Rupam—sitting tired and scared on the edge of the stage with Miss Whitfield. The Banker looked down sadly at the body of his daughter, still lying on the auditorium floor.

"I don't think she's badly hurt," Rich reassured him. "They said the wound wasn't too bad. But she's out for the count and she needs treatment." He beckoned them back into the relative safety of the storeroom and explained his plan.

"Only trouble is," he finished, turning to the Banker, "if they get you, they get all the magic account numbers and the money."

"Actually, they don't," the Banker said.

"What do you mean?" asked Jade.

"I don't have the numbers and pass codes. Well, not in their entirety. It's a safety measure, and it's why Mr. Ardman is so frustrated with me. I only know half of each piece of information. Ardman needs the other half, and that will only arrive when I'm sure I am safe."

"So these people, the Tiger's gunmen, if that's who they are, will only get half the information from you if you're caught," Rich said. "Who knows the other half?"

Jade and Rich looked at each other, realizing the answer at the same time.

The Banker nodded. "We each know half. We work together, out of necessity. Though there is one fail-safe, one place where we have stored the entire numbers and codes." He smiled. "Don't worry, it's very safe."

There was a noise from below—the auditorium door opening and then the sound of the large Scotsman's voice. They all turned to listen, but all Jade could make out was the distinctive burr of the man's accent.

"Getting any of this?" she mouthed at Rich.

He shook his head.

"Hang on," Jade whispered. She tiptoed back through to the gallery and lay down on the floor, pressing her ear to the bare boards of the balcony. The Scotsman was right underneath, talking quietly to the gunman on guard.

"You said it would be easy. Quick in and out," the gunman was saying. He sounded like he might be from Scandinavia.

"I know what I said." There was anger in the leader's voice. "But I was wrong. We can discuss it later, if you want."

"No," said the gunman hurriedly.

"Wise choice. But we need to get a move on. Won't be long

before parents are worried and calling the real police, never mind Hano and Danny at the main gates."

"Some of the children have been asking for the toilet."

"Oh, God help us," Red Beard said. "Right, that does it. I've got Masro looking for a public-address system. But we'll walk through shouting if we have to. Flush him out that way."

"Shouting what?"

"That if the Banker doesn't give himself up, we start shooting our hostages," Red Beard replied.

Jade heard the gasp of astonishment from the guard. "But they are children."

"Then we start with the woman."

"You can't kill children," the other man said, horrified.

There was a slight pause. Jade thought maybe the Scotsman was considering this. But maybe he was just glaring at his subordinate. "Watch me," he said.

Rich was better at throwing than Jade. He'd suggested a paper airplane. She told him to get real—it could end up anywhere. So instead, he wrote on a sheet torn from a pad in the storeroom, then wadded it into a tight ball.

"I just hope Gemma realizes what I'm up to," he said.

Jade shrugged. "She's *your* girlfriend."

"No, she's not!" Rich protested.

"Oh, come on—the way you hang out together. All the time."

"Oh, like you and Mike Alten, I suppose."

Jade smiled. "Yeah, right. Hit a nerve, did I?"

"You couldn't hit an elephant," Rich shot back.

"I'll tell Gemma you called her an elephant," Jade warned him.

Rich made his way tentatively to the front of the gallery. The guard was underneath and so couldn't see him. But the people on the edge of the stage could. Gemma was looking right at him. Miss Whitfield was glaring—like she was telling him off for sneaking away.

He held up the ball of paper and mimed throwing it to Gemma. Then he pointed down at the floor—toward the guard—and opened his hands in a theatrical gesture of bewilderment. Could he throw the paper—was the guard watching?

Gemma looked from Rich to the guard and back again. She gave no sign that it was safe, so he guessed it wasn't. He'd just have to wait—but for how long?

Miss Whitfield got down from the edge of the stage and walked briskly across toward the guard. For one awful moment, Rich thought she was going to tell him that there was a boy on the gallery who ought to be down in the auditorium with them and what was he going to do about it?

"What are you doing?" the guard demanded. "Back on the stage with the children, now!"

"Not until you tell me how much longer we are to be kept here," Miss Whitfield replied, in her telling-off voice. All trace of nerves seemed to be gone. "Some of the children need the toilet, and this young lady needs proper medical attention. I've done what I can, but she's lost a lot of blood. Look."

The guard appeared from under the gallery as Miss Whitfield led him to where the woman—Eleri—was still lying on the floor. There was a blazer folded up under her head now. If it were not for the bullet holes in her coat and the blood, she could almost be peacefully sleeping.

As soon as the guard was looking at the wounded woman and away from the stage, Gemma's hands came up, ready for the catch. Rich threw the ball of paper. Gemma grabbed at it. It bounced out of her hands and fell to the floor, out of reach.

Gemma glared at him like it was his fault. Then, in a single swift motion, she was off the stage, scooping up the ball of paper and pulling herself back up.

When the guard straightened up and turned to check on his prisoners, he could see nothing amiss. Rich just hoped Gemma would get a chance to read his message and would understand what he wanted her—and the others—to do when the time came.

If not, they might all end up dead.

15

"So what do we call you?" Jade asked the Banker. "I mean, 'sir' sounds a bit formal given what's going on. And I guess you're not really Mr. Argent."

Rich had returned to the storeroom. He was holding a stapler. "Maybe we need a code name," he suggested.

"Oh, right," Jade said, unimpressed. "What are you going to do with that?" She pointed to the stapler. "Staple us all together so we don't get lost?"

"Why not call me Dom?" the Banker suggested before Rich could reply.

"Is that a code name?" Rich asked. "The initials stand for something, maybe?"

"It's short for Dominic. That's my real name."

"Oh."

"Right, well, you and Dom . . ." Jade hesitated over the name. It didn't really seem to suit the man, and she wondered if it really was his name. Not that it mattered. Not that she cared, really. "Tell you what, why don't we just call you Mr.

Argent so we don't get confused? You get on with your distraction tactics and I'll get the phone."

"I'm not sure why it has to be me that does it," Mr. Argent said nervously.

"Because it's you they're after," Rich said. "If one of *us* pokes their nose around the door, they couldn't care less. They might even shoot us. But they want *you*, and they want you alive."

"And because I'll be quicker than you getting the phone," Jade said. She glanced down at her flat school shoes. At least she didn't wear heels like some of the girls. But she'd rather be in her sneakers.

"All right, then," the Banker agreed. "Let's get it over with."

"That's the spirit." Rich patted him on the back. "Come on, we'll be fine. It'll soon be over." He turned to Jade. "Will you be okay?"

"Course I will." She tried to sound confident. But her stomach was churning with anxiety—for herself and for Rich. "Look after yourself."

"Don't worry about me." Rich grinned.

"Of course I worry about you," Jade murmured as Rich and the Banker disappeared down the stairs.

The reception foyer was empty. Rich waited for several seconds at the end of the corridor, listening for any sounds that might suggest one of the gunmen was coming. But there was nothing.

"Okay," he said to Mr. Argent. "You're on. I'm all set." He brandished his stapler.

The Banker nodded and swallowed. "Right. Here we go."

He walked briskly across to the double doors that led into the school hall and reached out for the handles. He took a deep breath, turned to smile nervously at Rich, then heaved the door open.

Rich held the stapler ready as the Banker stepped into the hall. Over the man's shoulder he could see the gunman turning. The man's face was a mask of surprise.

Then the doors were closing again as the Banker turned and ran. He skidded past Rich and pressed himself hard against the wall of the corridor behind him.

Moments later, the hall doors sprang open again. The gunman stood there, looking around, searching for any clue as to which way the Banker had gone.

"Bannock!" he yelled. "Here—he's here!"

Rich hurled the stapler. Not at the gunman, but at the glass cabinet full of trophies. It stood close to where another corridor came into the reception foyer. The stapler smashed into the front of the cabinet, shattering the glass with a tremendous noise. A large silver cup fell from its shelf and bounced to the floor.

The gunman swung around in an arc, bullets spraying. The sides and top of the cabinet disintegrated. Then the gunman ran, heading for the corridor—away from where Rich and the Banker were hiding. Rich gave the Banker a thumbs-up and they crept slowly away.

Rich kept watching the gunman as they silently retreated. The gunman looked around, torn between following the Banker and staying with his prisoners. "Bannock!" he yelled again.

There was the sound of running feet now. But it was coming from behind them—from farther down the corridor where Rich and the Banker were hiding.

"In here!" the Banker whispered. He had a door open, and he and Rich pressed inside a small storage cupboard.

Rich's feet caught on something on the floor and he almost fell. The Banker grabbed his arm, saving him. "Sorry—should have warned you about that."

Booted feet tramped past outside. The cupboard was pitch black.

"Why? What is it?" Rich whispered.

"One of the gunmen," the Banker replied quietly.

"What?" Rich hissed.

"He had a run-in with your sister."

Bannock and two other men ran into the main reception foyer. The area was covered in glass, and the gunman from the auditorium was standing in the middle of it.

"He was here. The Banker. Went down that corridor," the gunman reported.

"You sure?" Bannock asked.

"Absolutely."

Bannock did not need to give the order. The two men who had come with him were already running down the corridor in pursuit. "Get back to the hostages," Bannock told the first gunman.

The gunman returned to the auditorium and pulled open the doors. He stopped in the doorway, staring in disbelief. "What the hell . . . ?"

"What is it? What's wrong?" Bannock ran to see.

The auditorium was empty. The children and their teacher—even the unconscious woman who had led Bannock and his men here—had all disappeared.

From the classroom next to Mr. Argent's, Jade could see enough of the corridor outside to know when the gunman left. She heard the shouts and the gunfire from below and hoped that Rich and the Banker were all right.

The gunman stepped into the corridor, looking in the direction of the storeroom—where the sound seemed to have come from. He hesitated a few moments, but then he went back into the classroom.

"Oh, great," Jade breathed. "A clever, sensible henchman. Just my luck."

In the darkness beneath the stage, Gemma had her arm around one of the younger girls to comfort her. Miss Whitfield was trying to make the injured woman comfortable. It had been a struggle to get her through the trapdoor—the teacher had been afraid that at any moment the guard might return.

But they had managed. Just. Now they were all huddled together, frightened and desperately trying to keep quiet. The girl Gemma was comforting suppressed a sob, her whole body shaking with the effort. The unconscious woman stirred and moaned in pain as Miss Whitfield did her best to soothe her.

The muffled sounds of angry men filtered through from the outside world. The furious Scotsman had found the open fire door in the wings, but another gunman outside the school seemed to be telling him that no one had come out.

They turned their attention to the balcony, but the Scotsman dismissed it at once. "No way they could get that wounded woman up there in a few seconds," he said.

"So where did they go?" the guard asked. He sounded even more nervous than Gemma felt.

"I don't know and I don't care. *He* was here. The Banker was here."

"Yes," the guard confirmed.

"Then the time for subtlety is over. I want each and every room cleared. Start again from here. Tell the others. A clean sweep, and this time we'll make sure no one slips through the net."

"We don't have much time left," the guard warned. "It can't be long now before someone outside realizes there is a problem."

"I know," the Scotsman growled. "That's why we clear each room with stun grenades."

Another gunman came jogging along the corridor toward where Jade was hiding. She pulled back into the classroom and hoped he hadn't seen her looking out.

He went into Mr. Argent's room next door, and Jade could hear him talking to the man in there.

"At last," she breathed as both men came out into the corridor and headed toward the storeroom at the far end.

"We'll start at this end," the newcomer said. "Bannock wants every room cleared. Start with this storeroom, eh?"

Jade crept to the door and looked out to see where they were. Sure enough, the two black-clad men were at the storeroom that led through to the gallery above the auditorium. But they didn't go inside. Instead, one of them pulled something from inside his black combat jacket and threw it into the room. Both men immediately moved to the sides of the doorway.

Oh, God—grenades, Jade thought, just a split second before the sound and heat of the explosion almost knocked her off her feet.

She ducked into Mr. Argent's room and ran to the desk. The pile of exercise books he had been grading had toppled over, so that the books were strewn across the desk. There was no sign of his phone.

From outside came the *crump* of another explosion. Jade checked under the desk, pulled open the drawers. She looked around, hopeless. There was a low cupboard full of textbooks and old exam papers and a tall filing cabinet, plus tables and chairs. Her own detention work lay abandoned on one of the tables. But there was no phone.

Another explosion—even closer—followed by laughter and a burst of gunfire. How many classrooms before they got back to this one? Another three? Or was it two?

With an angry gesture, Jade swept the exercise books off the desk and revealed the phone lying beneath them. She almost laughed out loud. Scooping up the phone, she ran for the door.

A quick glance told her the men were preoccupied with grenade-bombing the next classroom. If she was quick, maybe she could get down the corridor to the main stairs at the far end without them seeing. She ran out into the corridor.

"Oi—you!" a gunman yelled.

Jade was only halfway there.

"Stop! Stop or I shoot!"

Three-quarters of the way to the stairs. She hurled herself onward and sideways as a line of bullets drilled through the wall close to her.

At the top of the stairs she paused only long enough to look at the buttons on the phone before she pressed them—star five five star. She held the phone to her ear and took the steps two at a time. A dial tone—then the bleep of the numbers going through. A ringing at the other end, thank God.

More gunfire came from above. Dust and fragments kicked up from the steps around Jade as they exploded.

"Answer, won't you?!" she yelled into the phone.

She reached the bottom of the stairs. Just as a dark brown hand grenade bounced down after her.

16

The black 5 Series BMW took the bends of the winding country road easily and swiftly. Inside, John Chance hummed along to the Bach that blasted from the speakers. The car had a large display screen showing on one side which CD track he was listening to. On the other was a map of the area showing his position. It was angled into a perspective view with little clouds above the skyline, despite the fact it was dark outside. It gave the estimated time to his destination as twenty-one minutes.

On the windshield, just above where the hood ended, a display projected onto the glass told Chance how fast he was going. It refrained from pointing out that the speed wasn't actually legal.

The main display changed and the music cut out to be replaced by the sound of a phone ringing. Chance's cell phone was attached to the car's speakers and a microphone by Bluetooth—automatically linking up as soon as he got into the car.

ANSWER CALL was the highlighted option on the display screen. Chance pressed a button on the steering wheel to take the call. He didn't recognize the incoming number.

At once the car was filled with the sound of gunfire, followed by a colossal explosion. Chance swerved, crisscrossing the road out of instinct to avoid the fire. But then he realized it was coming from the speakers in the car doors—from the other end of the phone.

There was another loud explosion. Then, above it, a voice shouting. A female voice.

A voice that John Chance recognized immediately.

"I don't know who this is or what the hell's going on," Jade yelled from the car speakers. "But we need help and we need it fast!"

The sound cut out suddenly. The perspective map display gave the car's time to destination as twenty minutes. The glowing digits of the display on the windshield gave the speed as sixty-five miles per hour as the car took another tight bend in the narrow lane.

John Chance's expression was grim and determined as he selected a speed-dial number from the phone list and pressed his foot down hard on the accelerator.

17

The grenade bounced at Jade's feet. She stared at it for a second, her mind and body frozen. Then, without thinking, she kicked it. It hurt her foot, but the grenade skidded off across the floor and Jade dived into the space behind the staircase, landing heavily. She could hear the booted feet running down. Then the ear-punching *thump* of the explosion on the other side of the stairs.

The phone was still in her hand, but it was dead—the screen cracked and broken where it had hit the floor as she dove for cover. Well, she hoped whoever it was had gotten the message.

Now she had to find Rich and Mr. Argent and tell them help was on the way. But where were they? Jade could head back up the stairs to the math rooms or she could make her way back through the ground floor to the main reception and the school auditorium. She summoned the courage to head back up the stairs. It was the quickest way back and she was desperate to see that Rich was okay. But no sooner had she stepped out from behind the staircase than she heard the sound of running feet coming back toward her.

"It's all locked up—she can't have gone that way," she heard one of the gunmen say.

"Must have doubled back," the other gunman agreed.

Jade pressed back into the space under the stairs.

"Could have gone either way," the first gunman said. They had stopped almost within sight of Jade. "You try up there again; I'll head this way."

"And if we find her? It's not some girl we're really after."

"She shouldn't be running around causing trouble," the first gunman said. "She was in his room, so she might know something. Shoot her."

The corridor was empty. There was dust and debris everywhere. Each of the math rooms they passed was devastated by the grenades hurled in by the gunmen.

"Pointless," Rich said. "This destruction is just completely pointless."

"They're getting frustrated," the Banker told him.

Only Argent's classroom was still intact.

"They knew you weren't hiding in here because one of them was guarding it all the time," Rich said.

"Let's hope they still think I can't be in here," the Banker replied.

"Let's hope Jade gets back here safely." Rich was disappointed to see she wasn't there already. He had half expected—and hoped—to find her sitting at the table finishing her detention work having sent out their call for help. But the room was empty.

From outside came the faint sound of someone running up the main stairs at the end of the corridor.

"Maybe that's her," the Banker said.

But Rich wasn't so sure. "That sounds like boots, not Jade." He looked out from the door. There was no sign of anyone yet, but he was more sure than ever that whoever was coming wasn't Jade. Then he heard a similar sound from the far end of the corridor—more booted feet.

"They're coming at us from both directions," he told the Banker urgently. "We need to hide, and quick. With luck, they won't search properly in here again."

The Banker was pale with fear. "Hide? Where?!"

"I don't know." Rich was looking around desperately. Outside, the two approaching gunmen were greeting each other—shouting down the corridor. The Banker was pressing himself into the narrow space behind the tall upright filing cabinet. He'd be fine so long as no one looked there. Or chucked a grenade into the room.

Rich could see only one possible hiding place, if there was time. But if the gunmen found him, he'd be trapped with absolutely no way of escape.

18

Whether the man was a real policeman or not didn't matter. Either way, he'd have to move. There was a small group of concerned-looking parents caught in the lights of Chance's car as it sped along the narrow lane. The policeman stood in front of the closed school gates, the dark driveway snaking its way up to the old manor house behind them.

Chance put the lights on full beam and hammered at the horn.

It was not until the car began to turn that the man in front of the gates actually moved. Then he realized the car was fishtailing, the back wheels biting into the roadway as it struggled to speed forward again. The man leaped aside as the wheels spun, caught and propelled the car forward—straight at the gates.

Chance gripped the wheel tight in both hands and braced himself as the car slammed into the metal gates. There was a tortured shriek of twisting metal as the hinges gave way. One gate slammed open; the other fell away from the gatepost. The car bumped over them, already doing twenty-five miles per hour, and powered up the driveway.

Through the cracked spiderweb of the windshield, Chance could see the school. He could see its dark outline against the night sky. The figures forming a cordon around the outside. Dogs. And the orange-yellow of explosions within the main buildings.

A black-clad man stepped out at the side of the driveway and raised a machine gun. He was all but invisible, but the infrared image on the car's main display showed him clearly in shades of green. The car swerved toward him as bullets spattered across the windshield, pinging off the bulletproof glass, leaving snowflake impressions where they hit.

Chance dropped down a gear and the car accelerated into the figure. There was a bump from above as the man was thrown over the car, bouncing on the roof. Then he was a dark motionless shape in the rearview mirror.

High above, Chance could hear the sound of helicopters. Too early for Ardman to have responded to his call, he decided. No, these were waiting to extract the raiders when their job was done. Or when they decided they'd run out of time—if they'd been tipped off somehow that Ardman was sending in the troops. But there would be time to worry about that later. For now, Chance's entire focus was on Jade and Rich, then—and only then—on the Banker.

The car turned off the driveway and onto the lawn at the front of the school. The roar of the engine mixed with the sound of the incoming helicopters as Chance headed straight for the main reception area.

She was just congratulating herself on having made it back up the narrow flight of steps to the math corridor when Jade saw the gunman. He was standing outside Mr. Argent's classroom. He turned just as Jade emerged into the corridor. It was the man who had been on guard in the room earlier—and he had seen and recognized her.

Swearing under her breath, Jade turned and ran back down the stairs. She could hear the thudding of his boots as he came after her, shouting over his shoulder to a second gunman to stay put and search the room.

She reached the bottom of the stairs and was out of breath. Too much running. She had to find somewhere to hide. Out into the corridor, past the English rooms. Maybe she could get to a science lab and find some acid or something else to use as a weapon? No—too late, she realized. She wouldn't have time.

She ducked into the next room, hoping the gunman hadn't seen. But almost at once, the lights snapped on. He was standing in the doorway, looking straight at her.

Suddenly there was the ferocious sound of engines from outside. Through the large window that dominated one side of the room, Jade could see helicopters with searchlights. A car was bumping across the main lawn, headlights flashing across the glass.

Faced with the choice of car and helicopters or the gunman now aiming straight at her, Jade made her decision. She grabbed a chair, held it out in front of her body and braced herself. Then she put her head down and ran straight at the window.

Chance was wondering where to start looking for his children when one of them exploded out of a window right in front of him. The glass shattered and Jade was rolling across the gravel path, a school chair spinning away. A dark figure leaped after her through the broken window, gun poised.

The car swerved again as Chance heaved on the wheel. He pressed down hard on the horn and the accelerator. The car skidded off the lawn and crunched on the gravel. Bullets went wide and high, and then the gunman was flying back through the window he'd come out of.

Chance leaned across and pushed the passenger door open. The metal was twisted and it screeched as it opened.

"In—get in!" he yelled.

Jade clambered inside. "Dad—they're after—"

"I know. I got your call. Put your seat belt on; this could be bumpy," Chance told her.

The car reversed rapidly backward, fishtailing on the slick grass.

"*You* got my call?" Jade asked, confused.

"Ardman's on his way. I hope," Chance said.

"Those helicopters aren't his, then?"

"Don't think so. They were here too quick."

"Where are we going?" Jade asked as the car moved back onto the drive at the front of the school and accelerated.

"To find Rich."

"Yeah, I guessed that," Jade said. "Only you're not allowed this way around the school drive, you know."

Chance gritted his teeth. "I'll assume that was a joke. Now, where is he?"

"Not sure," Jade admitted. "Best bet is to ask at reception."

Behind them, the first of the helicopters was coming in to land on the lawn. Ahead of them, main reception was getting closer and larger. The car bumped painfully on the steps leading up to the doors. Then it smashed through the front of the building and skidded to a halt on the polished wood floor.

A man holding a machine gun was staring in disbelief at the battered black BMW in the foyer. He recovered, raising the gun. But before he could use it, Chance leaned out of the broken side window of the car, whipped out a pistol and shot him.

"Pity about your car," Jade said as she climbed out and joined her dad by the gunman's body.

The gunman was clutching his leg where the bullet had hit him and moaning with pain. Chance kicked his gun out of reach and turned away.

"Oh, it's not mine," he told Jade. "Company car. Anyway, the ashtrays needed emptying."

Bannock was in radio contact with the choppers, on the only micro-frequency they weren't jamming.

"The Tiger's got word that the security forces are on their way," he told the gunman standing outside the math classroom. "The others are on their way up here now. And the choppers are coming in."

As he spoke, the first helicopter dropped slowly past the window to land on the lawn outside.

"Have we found him?" the gunman asked.

"No," Bannock snarled. "So we take everything from this room—all his books papers, everything. Even if it looks like schoolwork. And pray we find some clue to where he is or where we can find the account numbers and codes before the Tiger has us all shot."

Bannock strode across the room. "That cupboard goes, and the books on the tables, and this filing cabinet." To make the point he dragged the cabinet into the center of the room.

His grimace of anger turned slowly to a broad grin as he saw the small frightened man who had been hiding behind it.

19

Jade led her dad into the school auditorium. "I want to check that Gemma and Mike and the others are okay," she said. "There's Eleri too—the Banker's daughter."

Chance looked around the empty auditorium. "His daughter?"

"She knows half the codes. Or something." Jade walked over to the stage and thumped the palm of her hand down on it. "You all right in there?" she called. "Miss Whitfield—everything okay?"

"We're fine," came a muffled reply.

Then another voice asked nervously, "Can we come out yet?"

"Best not," Chance called back. "Give us a few minutes, but everything's under control. We'll have you out of there soon, don't worry."

"Thank goodness for that," Miss Whitfield's voice replied. "This young lady has lost a lot of blood. And Lance is rather desperate for the loo."

"Oh, miss," a tiny voice squeaked. "You didn't have to tell them that!"

From the foyer outside came the sound of running feet and a bump like heavy furniture being knocked into a door frame.

"Are they evacuating?" Jade asked.

Dad gestured for her to stay quiet. "They've got us outnumbered—we have to be careful."

"We'll never find Rich. He'll be hiding."

"You're right. Our best bet is to stop the helicopters from taking off again. Or at least delay them till Ardman's team arrives." Dad had opened one of the double doors a crack and was peering out.

"They've got a filing cabinet and a cupboard. Taking all the Banker's papers and stuff, I guess."

"And Rich?"

He shook his head. "No sign. I expect he's holed up tight somewhere safe." He pulled the door fully open. "Right—all clear. They're on their way out."

Chance walked out of the shattered remains of the school front entrance, surveying the scene outside. Jade ran to join him. A second helicopter had landed close to the first. They were in time to see the man with the red beard—Bannock—climbing in. The filing cabinet and cupboard were loaded after him. So that was the one to go for. "Bullet in the fuel tank ought to do the trick," Chance murmured.

As he stood there, more lights appeared. Two pairs of bright headlights were bouncing rapidly toward the helicopters as cars raced across the lawn. The first helicopter was already rising, the massive rotors lifting the machine noisily into the air. Chance braced himself, feet apart, and took careful aim at the one still on the ground.

Two police cars suddenly swerved around the second helicopter. One of them slammed to a halt, blocking Chance's line of fire. The second accelerated toward the school and skidded to a halt on the driveway, sending gravel flying.

The second helicopter was lifting now. Soon Chance would have a clear shot at it. But before he could take aim again, uniformed policemen leaped out of the nearest car. They took cover behind the open car doors, aiming their handguns—at Jade and her father.

"Armed police officers! Put down your weapon and keep your hands where we can see them. You have five seconds to comply or we will fire. This is your only warning."

"But the helicopter's getting away!" Jade yelled back at them.

"I'm an armed officer with the Security Services, executing my duty," Chance shouted.

"We'll be executing *you* if you don't drop the gun," the policeman yelled back. "Hands on head—now! Or we fire."

"I'm telling you—"

"Now!"

He dropped the gun and put his hands on his head. Jade sighed and did the same. "Idiots," she muttered.

"They're just doing their job," Dad said. "Ardman called the local police and told them to send an armed response unit. They haven't a clue what's going on or who we really are."

Behind the police cars, the helicopters disappeared into the night.

"I'm sorry," Ardman said as he dismissed the policeman who had been standing guard over Jade and her father for the last half hour. Ardman produced a pocketknife and cut the plastic ties that secured Jade's hands behind her back. Then he moved on to her dad.

"You'd think they could tell I was a schoolgirl," Jade complained. "Have you found Rich yet? Is he all right?"

"We've searched the school from top to bottom. I'm sure there are places we've missed, but if Rich is there—we haven't found him. I'm sorry."

Jade looked away.

"And the Banker?" Dad asked.

"No sign of him either. As I say, there are still places to check. But if they were here and still . . . conscious . . ." Ardman shrugged. "Well, they'd have heard what's going on—the sirens, officers shouting for them."

"So where are they?" Jade demanded. "They can't just have vanished."

"They must have been on that first helicopter," Dad said. His voice was strangely flat. "The Tiger has them. The Banker and Rich—he's got them both."

20

The noise was incredible. Rich found it impossible to get comfortable and had to keep shifting positions, so he was glad no one would be able to hear him. He had not picked the best hiding place, he thought, but then, there had not been a lot of choices.

He had heard the gunmen come into the room and listened to the muffled voice of the big bearded Scotsman. He'd heard the Scotsman's delight at finding the Banker cowering behind the filing cabinet on the far side of the room and prayed that they would stop searching now and just leave. Despite Mr. Argent's predicament, Rich had almost cried with relief that it was all over.

Then he had nearly cried out in surprise and frustration as his whole dark world shifted. He could hear the two gunmen lifting him, swearing at the weight they had to lift.

"What the hell's he got in here?" one of them complained.

"Don't know," the other one said. "But you heard Bannock—we take everything."

There was some light through a tiny crack where the double doors of the low cupboard met, but not enough to see anything much. Rich was aware only of the motion as he was bounced down the stairs. Then he was lifted again and carried outside. The air was suddenly colder and the noise of the helicopters was louder.

"Oh no," he breathed. "Please, no." If he banged on the inside of the cupboard, would they let him go? But he'd seen what the gunmen and their leader—Bannock—were capable of. He even knew the man's name. Probably they'd just shoot him.

As he felt himself being lifted into the helicopter, Rich started to panic in the claustrophobic darkness and hammered on the doors of the cupboard. Of course, no one could hear him above the engines. And only now did Rich realize that when the doors had clicked shut, there was no easy way to open them from inside.

When he felt the helicopter lifting, he knew it was no good. If they found him now, they'd either take him with them or they'd dump him out the door. In flight. Better to stay put, stay hidden and hope for a chance to escape. After all, it wasn't all bad, he tried to convince himself—he was infiltrating the villains' stronghold. Soon he would know where they were holding the Banker. Then all he needed to do was escape and get a message to Dad or Ardman. Yeah, right—that was all.

The only light came when he pressed the illumination button on the expensive watch that Ralph had given him in

Venice—it seemed a lifetime ago. The movement of the heli-copter was making him feel distinctly ill.

And the only thing worse than being thrown out of a heli-copter, Rich thought, would be throwing up inside a cramped cupboard in a helicopter. He swallowed hard and closed his eyes.

They called it "the Wagon." It looked just like a large black van, the nondescript exterior giving no clue as to what was housed inside.

Jade looked around in astonishment. Down each side of the van was a workbench, and on each bench was a mass of equipment—computers, radar, headphones, and screens showing data feeds, CCTV footage, even the pictures from traffic cameras.

There was barely room to walk between the workbenches. Two men sat in small swivel chairs. They were constantly mov-ing—turning and wheeling up and down to check equipment, read from screens, type rapidly on various keyboards. One had hair to his shoulders, while the other had a military crew cut.

Ardman stood close to one of the men. He beckoned Jade and her father into the van.

"Sorry there isn't much space. But then, Alan and Pete here aren't that keen on company, are you?"

"Slows us down," the long-haired one said without looking up from the screen he was watching.

"Got a link to Fylingdales," said Crew Cut. "Patching it

into the satellite images to double-check." He clapped his hands together and leaned back in his chair. "Got 'em," he announced.

"Where are they headed, Pete?" Dad asked. He was having to stoop to avoid knocking his head on the roof of the van.

"Targets designated Bandit Zero One and Bandit Zero Two," the man with long hair—Alan—answered instead. "I'm passing their locator keys to the RAF. They have Tornadoes available."

"Time to intercept, eleven minutes," Crew Cut Pete announced. "Near enough. If they're on their toes, and they usually are."

"Intercept?" Jade looked at her dad. "They're not going to shoot them down, are they?"

"They'll escort them to the nearest RAF base," Ardman told her. "Though we have to assume the men in the helicopters won't like that."

"Not a lot they can do about it," Alan said. "We have radar locked on, and the bird's giving us real-time infrared. We can even count the number of people on board if I can cancel out the engine flare."

"We have Tornadoes in the air," Pete announced. He turned a screen slightly, and Jade could see three fighter planes streaking off a runway and rising rapidly into the night sky. The picture was a washed-out greenish monochrome, and she guessed that too was infrared. "Time to intercept, nine and a half minutes."

"They're changing course," Alan said. "Turning north."

On the screen in front of him, tiny pale helicopters were swiveling as they flew onward. Then the screen flickered and the picture disappeared. Blackness.

"What's happened?" Ardman demanded.

"Lost the feed." Alan was frantically typing into the keyboard. "Satellite's fine. I'm getting pinged back. It's still there and still sending. The fault's local."

"You mean here in the van?" Jade asked.

"I mean London." He sat back and sighed. "Diagnostics all check out. There's no problem. Well, no technical problem."

"Radar's gone too," Pete said. "Again, no technical fault. It's a reroute. Priority cutout. Looks like it's your problem, Mr. Ardman, not ours."

"You've lost them?" Jade said.

"'Fraid so," Pete replied. "RAF boys might get a local contact, but they're flying blind. Whole system's been whitewashed."

"Whitewashed? What's that mean?" Jade asked.

"This equipment does more than most people know," Dad told her. "The satellites give us far more detailed and close-up information than we let on. If someone hacks into the system, it resets to the minimum anyone would expect, just until the hacker is purged from the network."

"That way, anyone hacking in won't see anything we don't want them to," Ardman explained.

"So, someone hacked in just as we were watching those helicopters?" Jade asked.

Pete laughed. "No, we're the hackers."

"What?" Jade said.

"That's what someone told the system," Pete went on. "We've had our access key canceled. Doesn't only lock us out, but it ensures there's no data being received at all. So we can't just re-access and watch a replay to see where they went. The satellite should be back online in about three minutes, but we'll probably have lost them by then. Till we can get new access codes authorized, we won't be able to tell it where to look. And whoever canceled our codes can probably keep us locked out for hours."

"Someone with pretty high authority. Someone who didn't want us to see where those helicopters went," Ardman said. "The interesting question is, who?"

"The same person who tipped off the gunmen that I was on my way," Dad said. "The only way they'd have known to pull out and evacuate was if someone told them their time was up."

"I'm inclined to agree," Ardman admitted.

"You mean like a traitor? A mole?" asked Jade.

"I was with Sir Lionel when I took your call," Ardman told Dad. "He's the minister with overall responsibility for my department," he explained to Jade. "Apart from him, only a handful of people would have known you'd called. I alerted Goddard and his team at once; that broadens it to a dozen more . . . Not much help."

"But if there's a leak, possibly a traitor," Dad said, "we have to play this very carefully indeed."

"Tornadoes are breaking off," Pete reported. "They failed

to make contact. Those helicopters were turning north when we lost them. But they could have kept changing course to head anywhere. I've sent up some air-sea rescue to cover the east; the RAF are sweeping the north. We'll get west and south covered as soon as we can. But I'm not hopeful."

"I'll work out the range," Alan said. "See if we can put a boundary on their journey. Though they might pick up different transport en route."

"Aren't you missing the important point here?" Jade demanded.

"And what's that?" Ardman asked.

"We've lost them. We have no idea where those gunmen have gone. Or where they've taken the Banker and Rich."

There was a binder clip holding a bundle of papers together. It had been digging into Rich's leg for ages, but he finally managed to move enough to pull it off the papers. He examined it briefly in the light from his watch dial. It looked about the right width.

The wires that folded back from the clip itself just fit between the cupboard doors. Rich twisted the clip, forcing the crack between the doors open—not much, just enough so he could see out. He had to twist awkwardly to get his eye close enough to the crack.

He could feel that the helicopter was descending. The change in the tone of the engine confirmed what he felt in the base of his stomach. The world bounced slightly as the helicopter landed. The sound of the engines faded and he could hear people talking, dogs barking, a heavy door sliding open. Rich hoped they didn't just chuck the cupboard out but braced himself in case.

The cupboard was lifted out. It was on little casters and was set down on the ground and dragged. It bounced and rattled, throwing Rich painfully from side to side. But he barely noticed. He was staring out through the crack in the doors. The world outside was illuminated by giant floodlights. It was no wonder the ground was so uneven; it was probably cobbles or stone slabs.

The cupboard turned as it was maneuvered through a doorway. That gave Rich a final look back toward where the two helicopters were standing. He could just see the frightened, pale Banker following—urged on roughly by the bearded Scotsman. And he could see that they had landed in the enormous inner courtyard of a massive medieval castle.

21

The Banker's real name was Dominic Fendelmann, but he had not used that name for years. He wondered what his headstone would say or whether he would end up in an unmarked, unknown grave. Probably quite soon.

Any hope he had that Ardman and his people could trace the helicopters had ended when Bannock radioed to ask for a radar blackout. The gunmen seemed confident and optimistic.

But once they landed, Bannock saw who got out of the two helicopters. "Where is Duncan?" he demanded.

"Haven't seen him," one of the gunmen said.

"Not in this chopper," another said.

One of the gunmen had been shot in the leg and had to be carried inside, a tourniquet wrapped tight about his thigh. It made the Banker wonder how his daughter, Eleri, was—had she been badly wounded? It was a relief to find she was not on either of the helicopters. But did that mean . . . ? He hardly dared to think about it.

"Idiots!" Bannock proclaimed as he led the way inside the

castle. "Let's just hope Duncan is dead. Then at least he won't be able to tell them anything."

Bannock led the Banker and the men carrying the filing cabinet and cupboard through a wide stone corridor. There were electric lights, and the stone floor was covered with a plush, rich carpet.

They stopped at a huge wooden door. Bannock turned the large key in the lock and pushed the door open. It didn't creak as the Banker had expected. Inside, he could see a large, comfortably furnished room.

There was a sofa and an armchair, a mahogany desk, and a large log fire burning in a massive stone fireplace. There was no window, but soft light came from elegant gold-leafed wall lamps. A painting hung over the fireplace, a portrait of a beautiful young woman in Victorian dress. She was half smiling, as if mocking the Banker as he stepped into the room.

"You'll be our guest for a while," Bannock told him, leading the Banker inside. He pointed to where he wanted the cupboard and filing cabinet. "So make yourself at home. Enjoy it while you can. There's a bedroom through there, with a bathroom. If you want anything, ring the bell." He pointed to a bell rope hanging down by the fireplace.

"What could I possibly want from you?" the Banker asked.

Bannock smiled, but the humor did not reach his eyes. They were dead. "Food, maybe. Some wine, perhaps. To tell us the account numbers and access codes before the Tiger comes to ask for them in person. Because he will. And believe me, you will want to tell him." Bannock turned to go. He paused in the doorway. "Just ring the bell when you're ready to start talking." The door slammed shut, and the key turned noisily in the lock.

The Banker had seen the castle illuminated by the floodlights as they landed. It was huge and forbidding. A massive stone-built fortress. Even if he got out of the room, he realized, he was trapped inside an impregnable castle. And the worst of it was that he couldn't tell them what they wanted to know. For want of anything better to do, he walked around the room. Then he looked into the bedroom—almost as big as the main room and equally luxurious.

Back in the main room, the Banker opened each of the drawers of the filing cabinet in turn. They contained student records and old exam papers. Nothing remotely useful. The cupboard was full of old exercise books and answer sheets kept by his predecessor at the school. But the Banker unlocked the doors anyway. He swung them open, expecting no inspiration or surprises from inside.

Then he jumped back in shock.

"Oh, er—hello," Rich said, climbing out of the cupboard. He looked around, blinking in the light. "Can I use your bathroom?"

22

Jade insisted on returning to London with her dad and Ardman. Neither of them tried to talk her out of it. She and Dad went back to the cottage to collect overnight bags. They both knew they'd be staying in London until they got news of Rich.

Jade shoved clothes into a backpack, not paying much attention to what she was grabbing. She changed quickly out of her school uniform and pulled on jeans and a sweatshirt. After a moment's thought, she put on the necklace that Ralph had given her in Venice. A memory of recent adventures with Rich. Of being together. She tucked the delicate glass beads out of sight inside the sweatshirt collar.

Ardman gave them a lift. He drove efficiently and quickly, talking on the hands-free phone almost constantly while Jade and Dad sat in the back and talked quietly. It was after midnight now, and the roads were quiet.

Jade told Dad what had happened, as well as she could

remember. Anything might be a clue, Dad had told her—any tiny detail seen or words overheard.

As they reached the outskirts of London, Ardman leaned back and said loudly to them, "Apparently, we have a lead."

"The helicopters?" Chance asked.

"No. One of the gunmen. Seems they left him behind. Unconscious. In a cupboard." He glanced back, a wry smile on his face. "You know anything about that, Jade?"

Agent Goddard was a tall thin man with a drooping mustache. "I put him in the holding cell," he told Ardman as soon as they arrived at Ardman's offices. "But he's a tough one. You won't get anything out of him easily."

"I'm sure we'll manage." Ardman was at his desk. Jade and Chance sat in armchairs nearby, all of them sipping hot coffee. It was a large office in a Regency building and furnished in keeping with its age—apart from the computer screen and telephone on the desk. "Who knows he's here?" Ardman asked Goddard.

"Well, the local coppers know we took him. No one else, so far as I know. Apart from the medic who stitched him up. Oh, and we've got a cover story out for the school."

"Saying what?" Jade wondered.

"Vandals—they broke in, trashed the place and tried to set fire to it. Lucky the local cops turned up and took care of them before they could do any more damage, eh?"

"Yeah. Lucky," Jade muttered.

"Tell me about the gunman," Chance said.

"Well, he's British and he's not talking. Don't know much more than that. Running his fingerprints, DNA and face through the systems. If he's sneezed in the wrong place, we'll get a match. We'll soon know who he is."

"But that won't tell us where they took Rich," Jade said. The whole thing seemed pointless. "Can't you make him tell us?"

"There are rules," her father said.

"There are indeed," Ardman agreed. "But I think this may be one of those occasions where we are justified in bending them."

"You're not going to torture him?" Jade said, horrified.

"Of course not," Ardman told her. "What do you think, John?"

Dad was looking grim. "This is a job for the Professor."

Jade had dozed off in the armchair. She woke to the sound of voices. Goddard was gone and a new man had arrived. He was dressed in a dark suit and had a neatly trimmed black beard that made him look slightly satanic. He smiled at Jade, and she shivered.

"This is the Professor," said Dad.

"Pleased to meet you," the Professor said to Jade. "With a bit of luck I'll be able to find out where your brother is for you."

"Are you an interrogator?" He looked the type. Jade could imagine him brandishing electrodes, and she shivered again.

"In my spare time I help out Mr. Ardman and his colleagues. But actually, I am a stage magician. I do mind reading."

"Mind reading? You have got to be kidding." Jade turned to her dad. "Tell me he's kidding!"

"No, really," Dad said. "He's very good."

"Oh, you flatter me, Mr. Chance," the Professor said. "Now, where's Goddard with that file?"

The painting opposite Ardman's desk was not a painting at all. The Turner sunset faded to black, and Jade realized that it was a thin screen. It showed a view from a camera high up in the cell where the gunman had been locked up. Jade recognized him as the man she had tripped. It gave her some satisfaction to see he had stitches in his chin and his face was bruised.

Goddard reappeared and handed a thin folder to Ardman, who leafed through it quickly.

"He's still not said a word. Not even asked for a lawyer. Like I said, he's a tough one. I wish you luck," Goddard added to the Professor.

"You need this?" Ardman asked, holding up the file.

The Professor shook his head. "Just give me the bare details."

It was Goddard who answered. "His name is Duncan Hayman. Ex-paratrooper gone bad. Now a mercenary. Been in and out of various African countries who'd have been better off without him and done quite a lot of business in Eastern Europe. Nasty piece of work. For what it's worth, he thinks he's clean. His fingerprints aren't on record, he somehow got rid of his army files and his mug shot didn't get a match on any of the usual databases."

"So how did you find him?" Chance asked.

"DNA. Bit of luck, actually. He got the flu while he was in the army. They sent a blood sample to identify the strain. Could have been anyone's, but it was Hayman's. From that we got his medical records, and they cross-reference with his missing army files. We managed to build up some background from that. Not a lot, but it'll have to do, I'm afraid. Rest of it is long gone."

The Professor was pacing up and down in front of Ardman's desk. He paused and regarded the man on the screen. "So, as far as he is aware, we know nothing about him—who he is, where he came from . . . nothing. Is that right?"

"Right."

The Professor nodded and turned to Ardman. "Give me two pieces of information about him. Nothing to do with the army or his criminal activities. The two most obscure things you have that you are one hundred percent sure of."

"You think you can break him?" Chance asked.

"I doubt it," the Professor said. "But with a bit of luck and a bit of planning, I think I can persuade him to break himself."

"But he's not just going to tell us where they've taken Rich and the Banker," Jade said.

"Oh yes, he is," the Professor said. "Now, Mr. Ardman, what have you got for me?"

• • •

They watched on the screen as the cell door opened and the Professor walked in. The door closed behind him, leaving the Professor together with the gunman—Duncan Hayman—in the cell. An armed guard stood just inside the door watching them warily.

The Professor's voice came through loud and clear from speakers behind the screen. "I need some information from you."

The gunman looked up but did not answer.

"That's fine. You don't need to say anything. I shall get what I want anyway."

The gunman looked away. "You'll get nothing," he said. "Do what you like. I'm saying nothing at all." He turned back and met the Professor's eyes. "I've withstood more than you can imagine in the most godforsaken places on this earth. A man in a natty suit won't get zilch out of me."

"If you say so. Now." The Professor clapped his hands together. "I just need to ask you two control questions first. Then we'll cut to the chase. That all right with you?"

"You do what you like. I ain't speaking."

"I know. You said that," the Professor replied calmly.

Jade turned to her dad. "What's he doing?"

Chance nodded at the screen. "We'll see soon enough."

On the screen the Professor was leaning forward and staring into the gunman's eyes.

"You won't hypnotize me, if that's what you're trying," the gunman said. But he sounded wary.

"That's fine. Just fine. No, not hypnosis." The Professor smiled. "That's rather old-fashioned in my profession now."

"And what's your profession?"

"I do a stage act. I read people's minds."

The gunman guffawed. "Oh, my God, they're desperate, aren't they?"

"Are they? You think so? You might have seen my act or maybe one like it. It's not really mind reading, of course. It's a combination of things. Psychology, planting seeds in people's minds and knowing how to read people's reactions. For example, if I ask you a question, you'll think of the answer. And everything you do, even if you try to suppress it, will scream that answer at me. If I know how to read your reactions, I know the answer."

The gunman stared at the Professor. "You're joking. You're mad. No one can do that."

"I really don't care what you think," the Professor said sharply. "Now, as I said. Two control questions first."

"I ain't telling you nothing." He folded his arms. "And you're not guessing it by some fancy trickery either. You want to know where the helicopters went? You won't get that from me."

"Actually," the Professor said, sounding very reasonable, "I'd like to know your mother's maiden name."

The gunman stared back, openmouthed.

"Thank you," the Professor said. He pulled out a small notepad and jotted something on it. "And now, perhaps you can tell me—"

"Hold on!" the gunman shouted. He took a step toward the

Professor, but the guard at the door raised a pistol and pointed it at the gunman, who backed off.

"And now," the Professor continued as if nothing had happened, "perhaps you can tell me the name of your first schoolteacher."

"You're mad," the gunman said. "You won't get anything out of me."

"Thank you. And now we move on . . ."

"That's just rubbish!" the gunman yelled. "You're kidding, right? You don't know squat."

The Professor sighed. He looked at the guard, then turned back to the gunman. "Don't insult me," he said, his tone suddenly severe. "Your mother's name before she married was Jefferson and your first teacher was Miss Jones."

The gunman stared. "That's impossible," he said, but his voice was weak and nervous.

"Now, where did the helicopters go? Where have they taken the Banker?"

The gunman was shaking his head. "I won't tell you. You can't know; you won't get it from me."

"Thank you," the Professor said. "That's everything I need for now." He turned to the guard. "Tell Mr. Ardman I have it," he said. The guard unlocked the cell door.

"So far, so good," Ardman said, rubbing his hands together.

"Is that it? Does he know where Rich is?" Jade asked.

"Oh no, of course not," Ardman said. "As you know, we provided the answers to the questions the Professor asked."

"So what was the point?"

"The point is," Dad told her, "that Mr. Hayman now believes we know where the Banker has been taken."

"So how does that help?"

"Wait and see," Ardman told her.

The Professor was smiling as he returned. "I think that went rather well," he said. "Let's see how our friend reacts. Give him five minutes to stew on it."

When the door opened, Duncan Hayman was ready and waiting.

"Grub's up," the guard announced. He was holding a tray with a plate covered by a metal lid and a Styrofoam cup of steaming coffee.

The guard set the tray down on the floor close to where Hayman was sitting on the bed. As he stooped, Hayman saw that the guard's holster, strapped to his waist, was unbuttoned—the pistol poking out.

Hayman leaped up and grabbed the gun. The guard turned quickly, but not quickly enough. Hayman backed away toward the door.

"You stay right there unless you want your head blown off." He quickly glanced along the corridor and, seeing it was clear, stepped out of the cell. The key was still in the lock, and he swung the heavy door shut.

"Enjoy your coffee," he said as he turned the key. He could hear the guard shouting and banging on the door, but it was muffled. No one would hear him unless they were very close. Even so, he knew he didn't have much time.

The corridor was a stark contrast to the bare concrete cell. It was carpeted and wallpapered. Pictures were hung at intervals, with wall lights over each. The back of the cell door, Hayman saw, was paneled wood that matched the other doors off the corridor.

The first door he tried was locked. He moved on quickly to the next—that was locked too. But the third door opened to reveal a plush office. Hayman immediately saw the phone on the desk. There was a nameplate too—**GEOFFREY CAL-THORPE**. He lifted the receiver and was surprised to hear a dial tone. But dialing the number just gave a protesting bleep. He tried zero and a female voice answered immediately.

"This is Calthorpe; can you get me an outside line, please?" Hayman said.

"Of course, Mr. Calthorpe," the operator replied. "If you hang up, then prefix the number with nine I'll authorize that for you now."

"Thank you."

The phone was answered at once—another switchboard. "Extension 222," Hayman said.

"Putting you through," a voice said.

The phone rang for a while before anyone picked up. But Hayman recognized the voice that answered.

"This is Hayman," he said.

"Where are you? Bannock told me that—"

"I may not have much time. Ardman's people had me, but I managed to get away."

The voice was angry now. "And you called me? Here? You fool!"

"No, wait—I had to warn you. They know."

"Know what?"

"They know about the Banker, they must know about you. And they know about Calder."

There was a pause. Then the phone clicked and the dial tone returned. Hayman could feel a prickling sensation at the back of his neck. Like a sixth sense, as if someone was watching him. He turned slowly—to find the man who had questioned him standing in the doorway watching. There was another man with him—broad-shouldered with short blond hair.

Hayman felt suddenly cold. "You—you didn't know about Calder at all, did you?"

The man with the neat beard smiled. "No," he admitted. "But we do now. I said you'd tell me what I wanted to know."

Hayman brought up the gun he had taken from the guard. "Move aside."

"I don't think so," the broad-shouldered man said.

"I warned you," Hayman snarled, and pulled the trigger. There was a dull click from the gun. Then he realized that it was all a setup.

With a cry of rage, Hayman launched himself at the two men, raising the gun like a club. But the broad-shouldered man easily caught his arm. He twisted it up behind Hayman's back, ran him across the room and slammed him into the wall.

Hayman slumped to the floor, his vision blurring.

He heard the man who had questioned him, as if the sound was filtered through water. "Thank you, Mr. Chance."

Then everything went black.

On the screen, Jade and Ardman saw the gunman slump unconscious to the floor.

"Why didn't he fire?" Jade asked.

"The guard removed the bullets before he let our friend escape," Ardman explained. "It seemed a wise precaution. Can't have nasty people running around the place with loaded guns, you know."

"Suppose not. So now we know—Rich and the Banker are at Calder." For the first time in ages Jade was feeling elated. "So, let's go get them."

"Well . . ." Ardman coughed. "There is one slight problem."

"What?" Jade demanded.

"I have no idea where or what Calder is."

"It's a . . ." Jade hesitated. "I suppose it could be a place, or a house, or a company."

"Or a person or a small country, for all I know." Ardman sighed. "But don't worry—we'll find out."

The door opened and the Professor stepped into the room, followed by Chance.

"Well done," Ardman told them. "Yes, very well done indeed. Thank you, Professor."

"My pleasure."

"But he didn't really do anything," Jade said. "I mean, there was no mind reading or anything. It was just a trick. Anyone could have done it."

The Professor laughed. "Oh, please—don't tell them that or I shall be out of a job." He turned to Ardman. "The man was telling the truth on the phone. It isn't a bluff." He turned to go, then paused and said to Jade, "It isn't all trickery, you know. You've spent a long time in the United States. You recently lost someone very dear to you and you're worried you might lose someone else. Your star sign is Gemini and you're not sure whether to cut your hair differently."

"Yeah, all right," Jade said, smiling.

"You once had a hamster . . . No—a guinea pig, wasn't it? Called Sam. And the first boy who kissed you was—"

"I said all right!" Jade told him. "Point taken. You're very clever. They should pay you more."

The Professor nodded and smiled. "And you're very astute. Nice to meet you, Jade."

As soon as he was gone, Jade glared at her dad. "You told him!" she accused.

"Not me." Chance smiled. "How would I know that stuff anyway?"

"Hmm."

Dad frowned. "And you've kissed a boy?"

"Hey, back off," she warned. "My dad wasn't around to set a good example, remember?"

Goddard entered and interrupted. "We're running a check on Calder, whatever it is. The number Hayman called was a reroute. Went through about four reroutes before it connected, all with different telecom suppliers and one at least outside this country. Very high tech. Very clever. It'll take us a while, but we should get the number."

"Excellent," Ardman said. "And how is the poor guard that Hayman attacked?"

"Back on duty now. Says he enjoyed his coffee. There is one small problem, though," Goddard went on.

"Oh?"

"Sir Lionel Ffinch's office just called. Sir Lionel wants to know why the police at the school think we have one of the gunmen in custody and didn't tell him. He's on his way over now. And apparently, he's not happy."

23

Sir Lionel Ffinch was a tall, lean man with thinning gray hair and a hooked nose. Jade took an instant dislike to him as she listened to the man telling Ardman off like a child for not keeping him informed.

"And so I have to find out what is happening inside my own department from some bobby on the beat!" Sir Lionel sputtered.

Ardman seemed used to Sir Lionel's manner and kept his face blank and unresponsive. "I didn't see any need to inform the minister who oversees my department," he said with no hint of irritation. "Not until we actually had some useful information from the man."

Sir Lionel grunted. His aide cleared his throat and said: "And have you? Any useful information, I mean?"

"Oh, good question, Quilch," Sir Lionel said. "Very good question there."

Jade didn't much like Quilch either—he was a smaller, dapper man about the same age as Sir Lionel with slicked-back gray hair.

"No," Ardman replied. "Nothing I would yet describe as useful, to be honest."

"Complete waste of time, then," Sir Lionel said.

"Which is why I didn't bother you with it, Sir Lionel," Ardman said quietly.

Sir Lionel made a noise in his throat that could have been agreement or might have been censure. Turning from the desk, he seemed to catch sight of Jade and her father for the first time.

"And who is this charming young lady?" he asked.

"Get lost," Jade nearly said. But she caught Dad's warning look and said nothing.

"It's my daughter, Sir Lionel," Dad answered for her. "Jade Chance."

"Really? Why isn't she in school?" Lionel wanted to know.

This time Jade did answer. She smiled as sweetly as she could manage. "Well, you see, sir, some nasty people came and blew up my school."

Sir Lionel frowned. "That's all right, then. So long as there's a reason. Thought you might be having one of those dreadful bring-your-children-to-the-office days."

"We have those," Quilch said. "The prime minister is very keen on them."

"Right, then," Sir Lionel said to Ardman. "Seems we've had a wasted journey."

"I'm so sorry," said Ardman levelly.

"You did suggest we should see the prisoner, Sir Lionel," Quilch reminded him. "Have an official word and all that. Offer him a last cigarette."

Sir Lionel sniffed. "Well, it would do no harm, I suppose. I'm happy to have a quick word with him. Spell out the trouble he's in. Organize it, would you, Ardman?"

"Don't underestimate them," Dad said to Jade when Ardman had led Sir Lionel and Quilch out. "Either of them. Sir Lionel technically only has supervisory power. He can't tell us what to do. But he can withhold our budget and cripple us if we step out of line."

"And Mr. Creepy Crawly?" Jade asked.

"Quilch is what they call a special ministerial adviser. So he's expensive, and I guess Sir Lionel thinks he's worth it. He and Sir Lionel were business partners before Sir Lionel went into politics. Angus Quilch still runs the company they set up—and a few more of his own besides. Sir Lionel resigned from the board when he was selected by his local party as a candidate. Bit of a shoo-in, really."

Ardman had returned in time to hear this. "I remember it rekindled all those rumors that he paid for his knighthood," he said. "Beneath that bluster, Sir Lionel is a highly adept politician, believe me. He doesn't miss much. He brought in Quilch as soon as he became a minister to make use of his—I quote—'outstanding skills and experience of a non-political kind.' That sparked accusations of cronyism. But between them they run the department very efficiently. In fact, it's about the only part of the Home Office that comes in on budget and actually does what it says in the job description." He sighed. "The downside of course is that Sir Lionel is always looking over our shoulders and minding our pennies. So we have to keep him sweet."

"Sweet?" Jade laughed.

Ardman smiled back. "In a manner of speaking."

"So we let him see Hayman to read him the riot act," Chance said.

"If that's what it takes to be allowed to pursue this, yes," Ardman said.

"Do you know what Calder is yet?" Jade asked. "I mean, it's been hours."

"I know," Ardman admitted. "And we're doing what we can—believe me."

Rich was bruised all over. He sat in an armchair in the Banker's luxurious cell and tried to massage some feeling back into his legs. He and the Banker were talking in whispers in case the room was bugged, while classical music played loudly from a CD.

"Mind you," the Banker said, "if they have gone to the trouble of hiding microphones, there may be cameras as well."

"In which case we're dead," Rich pointed out. "Not that we're in great shape as it is."

"They don't know that you're here. That has to be to our advantage."

"It would be if I wasn't stuck in this room," Rich agreed.

"If I can get out somehow, I can go for help. Call Ardman and tell him where we are."

"But we don't know where we are," the Banker said. "Apart from being inside a castle, we could be anywhere."

"We won't find out just sitting around." Rich experimented with walking slowly around the room and found that the numbness was fading from his legs. They ached like hell, but he could walk. If he had to, he could probably run.

"There are no windows," the Banker said. "The only way out is that door, and it's locked. I think there may be a guard outside too."

"But they don't know I'm here," Rich reminded him, still whispering.

"How does that help?"

"From what you said, you can't tell Bannock what he wants to know because you don't know yourself, right?"

"Right."

Rich grinned. "So ask to see him and tell him that."

"But he won't believe me!"

Rich shrugged. "Doesn't matter. Trust me."

Sir Lionel and Quilch both seemed a little more understanding after they had met the prisoner. "Unresponsive fellow," Sir Lionel said. "Good luck with him."

"Obviously, you will let us know the moment you discover anything germane," Quilch added.

"Obviously," Ardman told them.

"Don't worry," Sir Lionel said to Jade as he and Quilch left. "I'm sure they'll soon have your school open again."

"Can't wait," Jade grumbled.

Her sarcasm was lost on him. "That's the spirit."

"I hate all this sitting around," Jade told Dad as soon as they were alone. "We need to be doing something."

"Nothing we can do," Dad replied. "Not until we know what he meant by Calder. That's our biggest problem."

"No, it's not," another voice said. Goddard stood in the doorway. "Where's the boss?"

"Just seeing Sir Lionel off the premises," Dad told him. "Why?"

"Our gunman is lying dead in his cell."

Dad wouldn't let Jade go with him. Not that she wanted to— she was still uncomfortable with the more aggressive and violent aspects of her father's job. Seeing a dead body was not something she reckoned was high on her list of things to do. But then again, she didn't want to be alone either.

She didn't have to wait long before Dad was back with Ardman, Goddard and the department's doctor.

"Definitely cyanide," the doctor was saying.

"If he had a suicide pill, why wait till now?" Dad wondered.

"Maybe he thought the Tiger would believe he'd betrayed him," Ardman said. "Once he knew we'd found out about Calder."

"Oh, I found a funny thing about that. Bit of a coincidence," Goddard said, grinning. His grin faded as he caught the doctor's expression. "I'll tell you later."

"What makes you think it was a pill?" the doctor asked.

"Simple to hide and to take," Ardman said. "Not unusual."

"Possibly," the doctor conceded. "But I'd expect some residue. He'd bite into the pill and crush it. Maybe it would be concealed as a false tooth or in a plastic shell under the tongue."

"So?" Dad asked.

"So, no residue. And from the speed and violence of his death . . ." The doctor paused and tapped his chin. "No, if I had to venture an opinion this early, I'd say he inhaled the poison."

"Inhaled?" Goddard said. "But where from? A tiny pill, he could maybe conceal, but we searched him thoroughly."

"What quantity are we talking about?" Ardman wondered. "Would it be in a spray? Or what?"

"A cigarette?" Jade asked suddenly as she remembered.

"Conceivably," the doctor agreed. "He would draw air in over the poison. It doesn't take a lot. Particles come too, particularly if the filter has been replaced."

"But he didn't have any cigarettes," Goddard pointed out.

"No," Ardman agreed. He nodded at Jade to say well done. "But Sir Lionel mentioned offering him a last cigarette. Goddard—check the CCTV footage for the last half hour."

"Already have, sir. But Sir Lionel and Quilch are sitting right in front of it, blocking the view of Hayman. It doesn't tell us anything, I'm afraid. Except what their backs look like."

Ardman's phone rang before anyone could comment. He went quickly to answer it.

"Yes, well, I'll leave that with you, then," the doctor said to Goddard. "But I'd check the cell and see if there's a cigarette end in there."

"Unless he took it with him," Dad said. "Did anyone see the man alive after Sir Lionel left?"

"I'll check," Goddard told them. "But you can't seriously believe that Sir Lionel is behind that man's death?"

"Believe it!" Ardman put down the phone. "That was Pete. He's traced the call that Hayman made."

"And?" Dad asked.

"And it was to the switchboard at the ministry."

"There's a lot of people at the ministry," Goddard said.

"Agreed. But the extension number of each call is logged by the system. Of course, we don't officially have access to that information. But Pete thought we might like to know that their data security could be improved. And that the call was put through to Sir Lionel's personal office. Which, gentlemen," Ardman continued, his face grave, "means we have a problem."

"Are you sure, Lionel?" Quilch asked.

"Oh, absolutely," Sir Lionel Ffinch told him. "You take the

rest of the week off. I can manage quite well. And I'm still a shareholder even if I'm not on the board. You toddle off and make sure the businesses are running smoothly."

"Well, just so long as you're sure it isn't a problem." Quilch still sounded dubious. "What with this Ardman business coming to a head and everything."

Sir Lionel smiled. "Oh, don't worry, Angus. I can handle Ardman, you know. And there are a few others matters that I'm hoping to give my personal attention to this week."

When he was alone, Sir Lionel pulled out a pack of cigarettes from his jacket pocket and looked at them thoughtfully for a moment. There was just one cigarette missing from the pack. "Yes, I don't think Ardman will be a problem," he said. Then he tossed the cigarettes into the waste bin.

24

The Banker hammered on the door until it was opened. On Rich's suggestion, he had first announced loudly that he knew the room was bugged and wanted to talk to Bannock. When nothing happened and no one came after ten minutes, they changed tactics, reasonably sure now that the room was not bugged after all.

Banging on the door achieved quicker results. The guard outside opened it and glared at the Banker. Rich could just see him from where he was hiding behind the almost-closed bedroom door.

"I need to speak to Mr. Bannock, urgently," the Banker said. "Take me to him."

Rich counted slowly to ten after they had left before he went to try the door. He had not heard the key in the lock, but he still let out a long breath of relief as the door swung open.

The castle was evidently a big place, and Rich was hoping there were not many gunmen around. But ever cautious, he kept to the shadows as he moved along the corridor, hoping he was heading back to the main courtyard where the helicopters had landed.

He pressed himself into a doorway as someone appeared farther along the corridor, stepping out of another room. But he went the same way as Rich—moving ahead of him along the corridor. Rich gave the man time to get clear, then continued.

After what seemed like forever, but his watch told him was only five minutes, Rich found himself at the end of the long corridor. There was a heavy wooden door with glass panels in the top. Through them, Rich could see the castle courtyard. One of the helicopters had gone, and the courtyard looked bigger than ever. If he simply ran across to the gatehouse on the opposite side, someone would be sure to see him.

In any case, he could see that the massive wooden gates were shut. There must be a mechanism somewhere to open them, but he had no idea where. And it was probably guarded. His only advantage was that no one in the castle knew he was even there, let alone running around free. He needed to keep that advantage.

There was a chance he'd find a phone, possibly even get an outside line. But what would he say—that he was in a castle somewhere but had no idea where? Big help. No, Rich's main priority had to be to get as far away as possible. Maybe there was another way out of the castle. Or perhaps he could climb down the outside of the walls. If he could get up on top of the ramparts, he could at least see the extent of the challenge that faced him and maybe get an idea of where he was.

He cautiously opened the door at the end of the corridor. Keeping close to the wall, he looked around for a way of getting up onto the battlements high above. He was in luck—nearby was a flight of steps cut sideways into the castle wall. It was early morning, and the sun was still low in the sky. The steps were in shadow, so there was a chance that no one would see him—or if they did, they wouldn't be able to tell who he was.

Trying to look like a ruthless mercenary gunman who had every right to be there, Rich climbed the steps. It was hard work—they were steeper than they looked, and it was a long way up. When he reached the top, he paused to get his breath back. Then he crossed the narrow walkway to look out over the battlements.

He stood there for a while, his mouth hanging open in shock. All thoughts of somehow climbing down or escaping from the castle and running for help . . . gone in an instant.

"You have got to be kidding," Rich said out loud.

"I'm sorry, sir, I should have realized." Goddard was looking embarrassed as he stood before Ardman's desk. "I thought it was a funny coincidence. But now, well . . ."

"What is it?" Ardman demanded.

"You've found it, haven't you?" Jade realized. She felt a moment's elation. Then it subsided as she remembered Rich's predicament. "You've found Calder."

"Have you?" Dad demanded. "Do you know where or what it is?"

"I think so, yes." Goddard went to a bookcase and pulled

out a map—one of a whole set of Ordnance Survey maps. He unfolded it across Ardman's desk. Jade joined her father and Ardman as they looked at where Goddard was pointing. It was a map of the north of Scotland.

"Calder is just here." Goddard's finger jabbed down at a point on the coast. "It used to belong to the state, but a small company has leased it in perpetuity."

"Can they do that?" Jade wondered.

"They can if a minister of the crown lobbies hard enough for them."

"Sir Lionel?" Dad asked.

Goddard nodded. "And that same small company used to be owned by Sir Lionel Ffinch himself. He still retains a large shareholding. Forty percent, I think."

"So what is Calder? A house?" Jade asked.

"Not exactly. It's a castle. Been there since the fifteenth century and incredibly well preserved. Sir Lionel's company had it renovated and made into a conference center with accommodations and even a helicopter landing area in the main courtyard."

"Helicopters," said Jade quietly.

"And you need them," Goddard said. He lifted his finger so they could all see that it had been covering a small ragged island just off the coast. In neat black print it was labeled CALDER CASTLE.

"An island," Chance said.

"The castle covers it entirely," Goddard explained. "There's a small dock at the main gates and the helicopter pad. Other than by boat or helicopter, it's impossible to get on or off the island."

Rich stared out over the battlements. He watched the waves crashing into the craggy rock on which the castle was built. He could just about make out the thin ribbon of mainland in the distance—across the churning, freezing water.

He felt the cold, salty spray on his face and knew there was no way he could get away from the castle to find help. He was trapped.

25

Ardman was holding a small war council in his office. Goddard was "disposing" of the gunman's body, so apart from Ardman himself, Jade and her dad were the only others present.

"We have to work on the assumption that Sir Lionel is the Tiger," Ardman said.

"Can't you just arrest him?" Jade asked.

"I doubt very much that I'd get permission," Ardman replied.

"And if he gets any hint that we are on to him," Dad said, "he'll make a run for it or have Rich and the Banker moved or both."

"We have to tread very carefully," Ardman said. "He keeps us on a tight leash, so it will be difficult to do anything without him knowing. Goddard tells me that we even need his signature to order paper clips. Now normally, we'd go ahead and act, then worry about justifying the cost afterward. But he'll be keeping an eye on us. A very close eye."

"But we *are* going to rescue Rich," Jade insisted. "We can't abandon him."

"Of course we can't," Ardman agreed. "But at the moment, it's tricky. As well as keeping tabs on the paper clips—or more importantly, any travel we authorize or equipment we check out—I wouldn't put it past him to have MI5 watching us. If we make any move, he'll know."

"Can't you do something unofficial?" Jade wanted to know. "Fly up there with guns and sort this Tiger out?"

Dad was shaking his head. "Authority for weapons on a plane would go through Sir Lionel's office. And even if we got there, as soon as we tried anything, he'd have it blocked from here. He'd insist we call it off. We use anyone directly connected with this office and he'll know about it." As he finished speaking, Dad glanced at Ardman.

Ardman was looking back at Dad, and Jade sensed there was something they were both thinking but not saying. "I'll go over Sir Lionel's head," Ardman decided, looking away. "Cut him out. With luck, he won't know. We've got enough circumstantial evidence to make a case for bypassing the system. If I go to Henderson in the prime minister's office, he can get the armed forces involved and Sir Lionel need never know. In theory we report to COBRA, the Cabinet Office emergencies committee, except they've delegated that to Sir Lionel."

"So, let's do it," said Jade. "What are we waiting for?"

"There are channels, formalities," Ardman explained. "It all takes time. The higher up the chain you go, the less time people have and the longer everything takes."

"Trouble is," Dad said, "we don't know how much time *we* have. It may already be too late. We need something now—something completely unofficial. Deniable. But in play."

Ardman frowned. "And if we're wrong about Calder, if we've misinterpreted the evidence against Sir Lionel, if we mess it up and come away with nothing . . ."

"Then we lose our jobs," Chance said. "More than that—we lose my son."

Jade had had enough. She stood up and leaned across Ardman's desk. "So—are you going to do something or not? We're just sitting around here talking, and God knows what's happening to Rich or to your precious Banker."

"Indeed, but as you see, our hands are tied," Ardman said.

"All I see is two grown-up men talking away and doing nothing!"

"Jade!" her father snapped. "That isn't fair. This is a very delicate and complicated matter."

"And what about you, Dad?" Jade went on. "I don't see you rushing to Rich's rescue. He got you out of Krejikistan and now you won't lift a finger to help him."

"Because Sir Lionel—the Tiger—is watching," Chance explained. "He knows I'm desperate to get Rich back. Hell, maybe that's why he was taken in the first place, as a hostage to ensure I'd do what I'm supposed to. Out of all of us, it'll be *me* he's watching to see if we've worked it all out yet and know where Rich has gone. Or he may already have had them moved from Calder—we just don't know."

"Well, maybe someone should find out!" Jade told them angrily.

"I think it might be best if you leave this to us," Ardman said. "Why don't you take a bit of time out? We're pretty central here—get some air. Go to a museum or the shops or something. But don't get involved."

"You mean kick up my heels while you drink coffee and do nothing?"

"We're doing all we can," said Dad. "I think Ardman's right. You need to clear your head and cool off. Try to see what is possible and what isn't, okay?"

She was getting nowhere here, Jade thought. She might as well get out. Do . . . something—anything. But she had no idea what. Not until Dad went on:

"And leave it to us, all right? The last thing we need right now is you charging off on some daft rescue mission. That's the sort of crazy thing Dex Halford would do. But I know you're clever enough to realize it would do no good."

The door closed behind Jade, and there was silence for several moments.

Ardman smiled. "It's risky, but I think that was very nicely done."

"Thank you," said Chance. "I just wish there was something else we could do. She's right—we just talk. Our hands are tied."

"I wonder if she realized we want her to go?"

"But I *don't* want her to go. Though I doubt I can stop her and we don't have any other options. I just hope she has the sense to let Halford take the lead. He'll at least be cautious until we can get a full team up there."

Ardman's phone rang. He listened for a moment, then turned to Chance. "Maybe we aren't so helpless after all. Eleri Fendelmann has regained consciousness. Let's see what she can tell us."

From the battlements, Rich could see there was a wooden dock outside the main gates of the castle. Beside it, a cobbled roadway sloped gently down into the sea. Perhaps long ago the castle had been on a hill but the sea had risen or the ground had subsided until it became an island. Or maybe the "road" was just an old slipway for boats before the dock was built.

Rich's best bet now was to try to get a message out. He might get lucky and find a phone, in which case he had to hope that "I'm in a castle on an island" was more help than just "I'm in a castle." He could try to signal to the mainland somehow. But there was no sign of life, and he could be anywhere in the world. What language did they speak, even? Failing that, it was message-in-a-bottle time. But for the moment, Rich decided to explore.

There were two armed guards close to the main gates. Another patrolled the walkway around the battlements. But all their attention was focused outside the castle, keeping a lookout for boats or helicopters. No one knew that Rich was even there, which made it easier to keep out of sight. But he knew that if he was spotted, he'd be locked up with the Banker if he was lucky or on his own in a bleak stone-walled cell if he wasn't No, he decided if he wasn't lucky, he'd be chucked into the sea.

With that thought in mind, he ducked back inside and made his way cautiously along one corridor after another. Eventually, he found a stone staircase. Up would take him to more rooms and finally to the top of the tower he was in. Down might be more useful.

He could feel a draft on his face as he reached the bottom of the stairs. This part of the castle seemed unused. There were no lights, just the sun filtering around a single wooden door. Rich reckoned he was at the back of the castle, on the other side from the main gates. He peered through the crack between the door and its frame and could see the sunlight on the water.

The door was locked, but it was neglected and rotten. A good kick and the lock broke away from the wood. The door creaked open and Rich found himself outside. There was a narrow strip of paving, then a drop of about ten meters to the sea below. Rich sat on the edge of the paved area, dangling his feet over the drop. The breeze and the spray on his face were refreshing. With the view over the water, Rich could almost believe he was back in Venice. Except it was bitterly cold.

He looked up and realized that anyone on the top of the castle tower above would have to lean right over the battlements to see him. He might not have found a way to escape or send a message, but at least here—for the moment—he was safe.

She was propped up in bed in a private hospital room. A saline drip was plugged into the back of her hand, held in place with surgical tape. Ardman had brought flowers, and a nurse had arranged them in a vase.

When he and Chance were alone with the woman, Ardman explained briefly who he was and what had happened to the Banker.

"Poor Father," she said weakly. "Do you know where he is?"

"We have a good idea," Ardman said. He glanced at Chance before adding, "Someone is on the way. We'll know soon."

"You are sure it is the Tiger who has him?" Concern as well as pain were clear in her expression.

"I'm afraid it seems very likely," Ardman admitted. "He'll want the account numbers and access codes that your father has."

Eleri struggled to sit up more. Chance reached across to help her.

"But he doesn't," she said, almost in tears. "He can't tell them anything. Father only knows half the information. It was always that way. As a precaution. If either of us was captured or taken hostage, we could not tell them where the money is or how to get it."

"He must know," Chance said. "There must be some way of finding out. I mean—what if one of you was hit by a bus? And how do you access the money when your clients want it?"

"It's automated. The computer system knows the account numbers, but they are encrypted. We have passwords to get into the system. But then we each have to enter our own personal codes. Of course we have a backup. The accounts and codes never change. There is a master list, somewhere safe. Somewhere only my father and I know about. Somewhere that no one would ever guess to look."

"Well," said Ardman slowly, "I know you've been to a lot of trouble to protect the information. But that information is a condition of our helping you and your father to start a new life. We need to know. If you can't tell us the accounts and codes, then you have to tell us where that list is kept."

Eleri bit her lip but nodded. "I understand. That was the deal. We give you the information and you freeze the accounts."

"So?" Chance prompted.

"The information is all kept in a secure bank vault in Zurich."

Chance had his cell phone out already. "Name of the bank?"

"Doesn't matter. It isn't there anymore. I took the list and I brought it with me. That was my agreement with my father. Once I was certain he was safe and you were keeping to our agreement, I would bring the list and also diamonds we had kept for emergencies. I took it from Zurich after I left Venice, when I was sure you were not double-crossing my father."

Chance nodded. "That was just a little misunderstanding with some old friends. Quite unrelated."

"So you brought the list here?" Ardman said. "You mean, you have it with you?"

"The Tiger's men found me. Followed me. I tried to get to Father to warn him and to get him and the list to you. But you know what happened at the school."

"But where is this list now?" Ardman wanted to know.

She looked up at them, eyes wide and moist. "I don't know," she said quietly. "I had it when I arrived at the school. The account numbers and access codes that you need, that the Tiger is so desperate to get hold of, are laser-etched into a large diamond, actually burned into the heart of it. Almost invisible to the naked eye unless you know to look for them. But they will show up easily with a magnifying glass."

"Let's hope the Tiger hasn't already got it," Chance said.

"Or if he has, that he doesn't realize the significance of that diamond," Ardman agreed. "If he gets that data, he could empty every account. Whereas if we get it, we can back-trace the funds and round up criminals and terrorists across the world."

"And if neither of us gets it?" Chance wondered.

"Then the money will simply stay where it is," Eleri said. "You won't be able to freeze the accounts, but you won't need to. No one else will be able to get at the funds, ever."

"We can't risk the Tiger getting that diamond. Under the circumstances," Ardman said, "let us hope the diamond is lost forever."

A large wave crashed down on the rocks below, sending spray splashing into Rich's face. It was cold and salty. He would have to move soon or he'd freeze.

Rich pulled a hanky from his pocket to wipe the water from his face. Something caught the light as it fell from his handkerchief and clinked across the top of the seawall where he was sitting.

The diamond sparkled as it bounced and spun. Rich grabbed for it, almost caught it, knocked it farther—right to the edge. The diamond bounced again—and fell over the edge.

Rich lunged and just managed to get his fingers to it. He fumbled and almost dropped it before clutching it tight. His heart was thumping as he held on to the diamond. So close! He had forgotten he even had the diamond and then, for an awful moment, he'd thought it would fall into the sea and be lost forever.

26

She didn't spot him until the Underground station. There was a train just about to leave as Jade came onto the platform. The doors were bleeping to warn they were closing, and Jade jumped on just in time.

A man she had not noticed must have been close behind her. He managed to get his shoulder between the doors as they closed. The doors opened again, and the man smiled an apology at the other passengers. No one said anything. The train pulled away. The man moved down the carriage, avoiding Jade's eye.

And she knew he was following her. Ardman must have sent him. Or possibly Sir Lionel. She sneaked glances at the man as he seemed to read the paper. But she caught the occasional quick look in her direction as he turned the pages. He was average height, average-looking, not young but not old . . . Just the sort of person they would pick—someone she wouldn't normally glance at twice or think anything of.

How could she get rid of him? After listening to Ardman arguing that they should do nothing to help Rich and the Banker, she didn't want him keeping tabs on her. The thought of Rich brought an unexpected tear to Jade's eye, and she wiped her sleeve across her face. What was Rich doing—was he all right? What would he do if he were here with her? Something clever. He'd have a plan. He'd know exactly how to get rid of this man—he'd have it all worked out. The teachers were right— she needed to be more like Rich.

The underground train pulled into another station. Jade was standing closer to the doors than the man. She moved aside to let people off. She stepped out of the train onto the platform to make way for a woman carrying a sleeping toddler. She could see through the window that the man was getting up, ready to follow, so she got back on the train and saw him relax and return to his paper.

Then as the doors started to close, Jade stepped out of the train again. She ran back down the platform, not looking to see if the man was following. If he wasn't quick enough, the train would leave and she would have lost him. But if he got to the doors again . . .

The doors finished closing and almost at once opened again. *I can do this all day,* Jade thought. As she passed the next carriage, the doors closed again. And Jade nipped quickly between them—back onto the train. He wasn't so fast that time. She saw him screwing his newspaper between his hands in frustration. She smiled and waved. He did not wave back.

Jade got off at the next station. As soon as she was above-ground, she rang Dex Halford on her cell phone. The number was busy. She waited as long as she could bear and tried again.

"Halford," a voice answered.

Jade breathed a sigh of relief. "Dex—it's Jade. I need some help. Can we meet?"

She was surprised to hear him laughing at the other end of the phone. "Yes, just tell me where."

"What's so funny?" she asked.

"Nothing. I'd just put down the phone, that's all. It was your dad. He said you might call."

Rich was cold. And despite the situation, he was bored. He pulled his school blazer tight around him. Here he was, sitting looking out over the sea, trapped in a castle on a tiny island guarded by men with guns, and he was bored.

He'd already decided there was no way off the island. He wasn't going to try to swim for it. He could see how far it was to the shore through the icy water. And even if he made it, he could be anywhere. He might still be miles—hundreds of miles, even—from civilization. He couldn't fly the helicopter and he was unarmed, so there was no point attempting a hijack. The only other option was a boat. That sounded good—he'd seen the dock outside the main gates. But there was no boat there and maybe never would be.

So, he could kick his legs and wait till he froze or got hungry or needed the toilet. Or he could—what? What could he do? What would Jade do?

She'd probably lose it completely, throw caution to the wind and trash the place. Rich smiled to himself at the idea. But maybe he should take a leaf out of her book. It would distract and annoy Bannock and his heavies, and perhaps if he caused enough trouble, someone on the mainland would see there was a problem and send in help . . .

Had to be better than sitting around getting cold.

It didn't take Jade long to explain the situation to Halford, and he suggested they meet at Heathrow. "We'll get a flight up to Inverness, but we'll have to drive from there."

It was a huge relief to Jade that he didn't argue—he just assumed that they were going to Calder to find and rescue Rich.

Jade and Rich both knew Dex Halford well—he had helped them get to Krejikistan to rescue Dad, and he had introduced them to Ralph. Back when they were in the SAS together, Dad had carried the wounded Halford out of a firefight behind enemy lines in Afghanistan. Halford had lost his leg from the wound, but if you didn't know, you would think he just had a slight limp.

"I know from experience I can't talk you out of coming," Halford said. "So I won't waste my breath trying. I'd do better to spend the time thinking about how to tell your dad you came too. Got your passport?"

"Er, no," Jade confessed. "I didn't think I'd need it."

"You'll need a photo ID for the flight," Halford told her over the phone. "But don't worry. I'll figure out something."

Rich followed his nose. His stomach was rumbling as he could smell bacon cooking. It occurred to him he'd not eaten since lunch the previous day. Since he was heading for the kitchen anyway . . .

There would be all sorts of useful things in the kitchen. Not just knives—though Rich doubted he could bring himself to use one in anger. But if there was bacon as well, then that was a bonus.

The kitchen was in the basement under one of the four massive towers that were situated at each corner of the castle. There was no reason to suppose the kitchen would be guarded, but Rich approached cautiously. He could hear the clatter of metal pans and someone whistling.

A chef, in white uniform and tall hat, was busy at a large stove. Rich watched from the shadows outside the door as the chef went about his business. Rich didn't recognize the man, but he could be one of the gunmen who had been at the school—if he saw Rich in his crumpled school uniform, he might raise the alarm.

After a few minutes, the chef was done. He had a plate ready on a tray and loaded it with fried bread, scrambled eggs, sausage and bacon. Rich was about ready to knock the man down and grab the food. But he forced himself to wait. Sure enough, the chef put a metal cover over the plate, then took the tray and left.

As soon as the chef was gone, Rich went into the kitchen. He waited just inside the door, listening in case there was anyone else around. But the place was silent and still. There was no bacon or sausage left in the pan, but Rich found a fridge and helped himself to bread and ham.

He found a small, sharp knife—which might come in handy for cutting through ropes or material. He found a half-empty bottle of white wine in the fridge and took out the cork. He pushed the thin blade of the knife into the cork until the sharp edge was completely covered, then put it in his blazer pocket.

More immediately useful was a large metal drum of cooking oil and a box of matches. Rich stuffed the matches into his pocket as well. The drum was empty enough that he could carry it, though the outside was slippery where oil had spilled. Before he left, Rich turned on all the gas taps on the oven.

The higher up he was the better, Rich decided. It was tricky getting the heavy drum of oil up the stairs. He paused frequently to listen for the sounds of anyone coming and because he needed to rest. At one point he froze as he heard footsteps from the floor above. But the steps continued on, not coming down the stairs.

Eventually, Rich was on the top floor. He rolled the drum along the carpeted corridor. Viscous cooking oil was leaking out around the cap, but that didn't matter.

The first room Rich tried was a bedroom. There was a phone on the cabinet by the bed. When Rich listened, there was a tone, but no matter what he dialed, he got nothing more. So he ripped the cord out of the wall and dumped the phone on the bed.

The next room was another bedroom. There was a book on

a cabinet by the unmade bed and another phone. He ripped out the phone, tossed the book under the bed and moved on.

An empty room with a window looking out at the distant mainland was the best option, he decided. Leaning out of the window, he could see the empty wooden dock and the cobblestone causeway underneath him. He must be right over the main gates. Rich left the drum of oil in the middle of the room and went back to the nearest bedroom to grab sheets and blankets. There was a magazine about cars by the bed, so he took that too.

Rich piled the blankets on the floor with the sheets on top. After some thought, he moved the pile close to the window and trailed the sheets out of it. They billowed in the breeze, and one nearly escaped and blew away. He wrapped them through the window hinges until they were secure. Then he tore the pages from the magazine, poking them in between the folds of the blankets so that the edges were still visible. With the pile complete, he emptied the drum of oil over the blankets.

It worked better than he had hoped. Rich lit the exposed edges of paper, and before long the whole mass of blankets was burning furiously. The sheets also caught, and the oil meant there was plenty of smoke. The breeze outside dragged the smoke from the room. Anyone watching from the mainland would think—Rich hoped—that the castle was on fire.

It was a faint possibility, but maybe, just maybe, someone would report it and a police launch would come out to the castle. Or something. Anything.

Daydreaming about the various possibilities of rescue and keeping well clear of the heat and smoke, it took Rich a while to hear the shouts from below. Of course—the guards at the gate had seen or smelled the smoke almost at once. With a last satisfied look at the roaring fire, Rich turned and hurried from the room.

Already he could hear people running up the staircase, so Rich set off the other way down the corridor. He rounded a corner and slammed right into a large man. Powerful hands gripped him tight.

Rich kicked as hard as he could at the man's shins. The grip slackened as the man grunted in pain, and Rich managed to tear himself free. He dodged around the man. But there was another man right behind him—Bannock.

Rich pulled the small knife from his pocket. But before he could even remove the cork, it was knocked from his hand and went flying. He kicked out desperately, but Bannock grabbed Rich's foot, pulling him violently off balance. Rich crashed to the floor. He felt a hand on his shoulder, rolling him over. He struggled to crawl away, but the hands lifted him back onto his feet. With one arm now pinned, Rich grabbed the only thing he could reach—Bannock's beard. He heaved as hard as he could.

Bannock guffawed with laughter. He pried Rich's fingers from the beard and slammed him against the wall of the corridor. Rich's cheek connected painfully and the pressure was so hard he felt he might burst and be splattered across the wallpaper.

"How the hell did you get here?" Bannock demanded.

The pressure eased slightly, so that Rich could answer. There didn't seem to be much he could gain by lying, though he wanted to keep the Banker out of it. "I hid in a cupboard, in Mr. Argent's classroom. And then someone put the cupboard on a helicopter. I managed to sneak out of it after the helicopter landed, but then I was stuck in this castle."

"So you thought you'd burn it down." As Bannock spoke, a man ran past them with a fire extinguisher.

"I couldn't get out," Rich pleaded. "I was scared. I was trying to signal for help."

"He's resourceful," the man Rich had kicked said.

"Too resourceful," Bannock decided. "You're not going anywhere, sonny. Except maybe back in the cupboard."

Bannock marched Rich to the room where the Banker was locked up. As he was thrust back into the room, Rich was afraid that Bannock really was going to lock him inside the cupboard again. His legs were beginning to ache just at the thought of it.

"Company for you," Bannock told the startled Banker.

Rich shook his head just enough for the Banker to see and know to say nothing.

"Might focus your mind," Bannock went on. "Because you know what? I don't believe that stuff about not knowing the account numbers and codes. Nor does the Tiger." He grinned at the Banker's anxious expression. "Oh yes, he's coming to see us. And when he gets here in a few hours, you'll tell us what we want to know. Otherwise, we'll kill the boy."

His grin froze as from somewhere below them came the rumble of an explosion, followed by shouts.

"Ah, sorry," said Rich. "That'll be your oven."

27

Ardman and Chance were waiting outside Sir Lionel's office when he returned from lunch.

"Gentlemen—what can I do for you?" He waved them inside.

"No Quilch?" Ardman commented.

"Oh, gave him some time off. Now, what are you two after? Found our elusive Banker yet, have we?"

Chance could detect the smell of wine on Sir Lionel's breath. He was a cool one, that was for sure. His funds had been wiped out and he might be about to be exposed as a traitor and criminal, but he still made time for a decent lunch. And keeping up the bluster was quite an act . . .

"We haven't, I'm afraid," Ardman said. "But it looks like that doesn't matter anymore."

"Oh?" There was a definite wariness in Sir Lionel's voice.

While the man's attention was all on Ardman, Chance took the opportunity to walk slowly across the office. He pretended to be examining a picture on the wall.

"The woman, Eleri Fendelmann, has regained conscious-ness," Ardman said.

"I wasn't told," Sir Lionel snapped angrily.

"Only just happened, sir. Quite by coincidence, Chance and I were at the hospital checking with the doctors."

"So what's she got to say for herself? She's this Banker man's daughter, so she probably doesn't know much at all."

"On the contrary." As he spoke, Ardman walked across Sir Lionel's office—away from where Chance was standing. Sir Lionel was watching him carefully. So if he saw Chance reach out and straighten the picture slightly, he paid no attention. Certainly he did not see the slim metal box that Chance pressed against the wood paneling behind the picture.

"Miss Fendelmann worked very closely with her father. She handled the day-to-day business and transactions for him. The Tiger has messed up royally, I'm pleased to say."

Sir Lionel seemed to be shaking with anticipation. Or anger. "How d'you mean?" he demanded.

"He should have taken the woman, not the father. She's given us the account numbers and the access codes. She's identified which accounts are legitimate business accounts they serviced as part of their cover and which are the ones we are interested in."

"So—it's all over," Sir Lionel said quietly.

"Just about, sir," Chance agreed. "Just a formality now. We need to freeze the accounts in case the Tiger does get the information. But after nine o'clock tomorrow morning it will be no use to him if he does."

"Well, well, well." Sir Lionel seemed to have recovered some of his composure. "Good job. All's well that ends well, eh?"

"Indeed," Ardman agreed. "I thought you would want to be told personally and as soon as possible."

"Thank you. Oh, just one thing," he added as Ardman and Chance made for the door. "Why nine o'clock tomorrow? Why the delay?"

"Legal formality, sir," Chance said. "That's the earliest we can get a judge to rule on the order to freeze the assets. Without that the banks won't release the funds, and technically the accounts can still be accessed till then."

"If the Tiger is hoping to get his money back from under our noses," Ardman said, "then he'll have to move fast."

The first flight they could get on was early afternoon. The check-in clerk looked at Jade's passport, then at Jade.

"What?" Jade asked. "What's she doing, Uncle Dex? What's the problem?"

The picture in the passport that Halford had brought didn't look much like Jade. But it was the only one his contacts could find for him that would do for a teenage girl. So according to her passport, Jade was seventeen, she was called Claire Reed, and she had long black hair.

"She's had her hair cut," Halford said to the clerk.

"It's dyed too," Jade added. "That's allowed, isn't it?"

"It doesn't look dyed," the woman said, staring at Jade's blond bob.

"In the *photo*," Jade told her. "I had my hair dyed when the photo was taken. God, you can see the roots if you look."

"Can we hurry it up, please, do you think?" Halford asked. "I mean, what's the problem? It's only an internal flight."

The woman said nothing, but she printed out the boarding cards.

The flight to Inverness was just under two hours, but then they needed to get a car.

"It'll be dark by the time we get to Calder," Jade grumbled as the plane lifted from the runway.

"That may not be a bad thing," Halford pointed out. "He'll be fine," he went on. "Your brother's a clever kid. He'll be okay."

"I know." Jade watched the ground dropping away. The plane rose through cobwebs of cloud. Her face was reflected in the plastic of the window—a blond-haired girl wiping her eyes and staring into the sky.

The Banker listened attentively as Rich explained what he'd discovered about where they were and what he had been up to.

"Bannock didn't believe me," he told Rich. "He thinks I'm holding out on him. Things will soon get very ugly, I think. Once the Tiger gets here . . ." He shivered.

"Haven't you met the Tiger?" Rich asked.

"No. Not even when he first employed me. It was all through intermediaries. He is a very private, very cautious man. But over the years I have dealt with him by phone and e-mail. Enough to know that he is not a nice man. He pretends to be. He is respected and has a direct line, some say, to the prime minister. But I'm not looking forward to our first meeting."

The door opened and Bannock came in. "I've just got word that the Tiger will soon be on his way here," he said. "He asked me to tell you that you have until dawn to provide the information we need."

"Or what?" Rich asked defiantly.

"Or we kill you. After nine o'clock tomorrow the information will be useless. *You* will be useless," he said to the Banker. "So you'd better think of a way of making yourself useful."

"Nine o'clock tomorrow," Rich repeated.

"Let's not split hairs," Bannock said. "We need time to use the information. So, let's say seven o'clock, shall we?"

The door slammed shut behind him.

Rich looked at the watch that Ralph had given him. It was approaching five in the afternoon. Outside, the evening would be drawing in. The clock above the mantelpiece gave the same time. "We must be in the same time zone," Rich realized. "We're probably still in Britain—Europe's an hour different, isn't it?"

"Doesn't matter where we are," the Banker said glumly. "The Tiger will be here all the more quickly and we have only fourteen hours left to live."

Keeping to his schedule, Sir Lionel left the ministry at 6 p.m. exactly. His ministerial car was waiting outside. The chauffeur climbed out and opened the back door for him. It was not the usual man, Sir Lionel noticed.

"Where's Lawson?" he asked.

"Off sick today, sir."

Sir Lionel frowned. The man's face was shadowed by the peak of his cap, which was pulled down low. "Don't I know you?"

"Probably driven you before, sir."

"Yes, that's probably it." Sir Lionel got into the back of the car and settled himself on the leather seat. He set his briefcase down beside him. "Home, then, please," Sir Lionel ordered. "And remind me of your name, would you?"

"Goddard, sir."

Sir Lionel felt a chill as he realized where he knew the man from. "But—you work for Ardman. In operations."

"That's right, sir." The car was pulling up already, just a hundred meters from the ministry.

"That's ridiculous. What are you doing here? Why are we stopping?"

"I'm on an operation now actually, sir," said Goddard.

"I've authorized nothing like this. Does Ardman know?" Sir Lionel demanded. "I shall have severe words with him."

"Right you are, sir. Actually, to save time, you could do it now."

The back door of the car opened and Ardman climbed in beside Sir Lionel, who shuffled across and grabbed his briefcase, ready to get out the other side. But that door opened too and Chance got into the car.

"This is intolerable!" Sir Lionel complained loudly.

"I quite agree," Ardman said darkly. "To the office, please, Goddard."

Sir Lionel opened his mouth to protest, but he felt something jab into his ribs. When he looked down, Sir Lionel saw that Chance was holding a pistol tight against him.

By the time they arrived at Ardman's office, Sir Lionel was livid "I shall protest in the strongest terms," he insisted. "Just wait until Malcolm Henderson in the prime minister's office hears about this."

Ardman ignored him. Goddard and Chance were standing behind Sir Lionel, ready to move in if things got nasty. Who knew what a cornered tiger might do?

"Please confirm, Sir Lionel, that this is your voice," Ardman said. He tapped at his computer keyboard and a voice said:

"Ah, glad I caught you. I've got some news I thought you might be interested to hear . . ."

Ardman stopped the playback. "Well?"

"Yes, of course it's my voice. But—"

"Just answer questions as they are put to you, sir," Chance told him. "That was a playback of your side of a telephone call you made this afternoon at 4:45 p.m. Do you deny making the call?"

"No, of course not." Sir Lionel was shaking with rage. "Am I to understand that you've been tapping my phone?"

"No, that would have taken too long to arrange," said Ardman.

"So we bugged your office instead," Chance explained. "That's why, sadly, we only caught your side of the conversation."

The playback cut in again. "It appears that Ardman has managed to get the account numbers and access codes that he needs. So the money controlled by the Banker will be frozen at nine tomorrow morning. After that, no one will be able to get at it. I don't have to tell you what that means . . ." There was a pause, then Sir Lionel's voice continued, "You too. I'll see you soon."

"And what does that mean?" Ardman said. "I think you owe us an explanation."

"I owe you nothing of the sort—what is going on here?" Sir Lionel demanded.

"Sir Lionel," Chance said quietly, "we gave you certain confidential information this afternoon. Very sensitive information that could be highly damaging. If it were true."

"What do you mean? It isn't true? We're not freezing the accounts?"

"I'm afraid not," Ardman admitted. "But you didn't know that. And you passed that information on to an accomplice. It is fairly clear from what we heard that you were telling them they had till nine o'clock tomorrow morning to get the information you need from the Banker."

"From the Banker?" Sir Lionel had gone very pale. He wiped his forehead with a handkerchief. "You cannot seriously believe I know where the Banker is when you've failed to find him?"

"Oh, come on," Goddard said. "Of course you know. Your people took him."

"My people?" Sir Lionel looked confused.

"The people you called to tell them to hurry up and get the bank data."

"This is ridiculous." Sir Lionel reached into his jacket pocket.

But Chance grabbed his hand and lifted it away. "Careful, sir."

"Check he hasn't got any cigarettes," Goddard said.

"I don't smoke. I was putting my hanky away."

"You don't smoke, Sir Lionel?" Ardman said. "But you offered our prisoner Hayman a cigarette, if I recall. You even joked about it. A last cigarette."

"Not so funny, as it turns out," Chance added. "Given the cigarette killed him."

"What?" The word was almost a shriek. "But it wasn't my cigarette. I borrowed them. Forgot to give them back, actually. The pack's probably still in the bin at the office."

"The office where Hayman called you?" Goddard said. "The office where you made that call we just heard?"

"I was calling Quilch. He's got some days off, but I thought he'd be pleased to hear the good news. That's what I was telling him—when I said, 'I don't have to tell you what that means,' I was telling him it was over. We've got the funds frozen and all our work has paid off."

Sir Lionel wiped a hand across his brow. "Do you mind if I sit down? I'm feeling a bit wobbly. Now you tell me it isn't true at all, and I haven't a clue what's going on." He walked slowly to the nearest chair and sank down into it.

Ardman and Chance looked at each other. "Hayman made a call from here," Ardman said. "To the Tiger."

"I know nothing about that," Sir Lionel said.

"He called the ministry—he was put through to your office. An hour before you and Quilch arrived here to see him."

Sir Lionel frowned. "But that means . . ."

"And we know that the Banker is being held on Calder. Which you arranged to be sold to your own company."

Sir Lionel was shaking his head. "Only forty percent mine. And I never wanted the damned place—it's too far out in the middle of nowhere to be of any use. That was Quilch's idea. He said it would save the heritage boys from having to pay for the upkeep. Give a little bit back. And for your information, an hour before coming here, I was in a meeting with the prime minister. I'm sure he'll remember, and if by some quirk he doesn't, it's in both our diaries."

"But then who took the call?" Chance said. But even as he asked, he guessed the answer—as he saw Ardman had.

"The same person as takes all my calls when I'm out of the office," Sir Lionel said.

The helicopter kicked up a cloud of dust as it settled down in the courtyard of Calder Castle.

Bannock was waiting to greet the Tiger as he stepped out

onto the flagstones. It always amazed Bannock that such a small, unassuming-looking man could control such power, such wealth. Could be so powerful and—even by Bannock's standards—vicious.

The Tiger straightened his suit. "We don't have much time!" he shouted above the noise of the rotor blades.

"So I gathered, sir. But we might have some leverage over our friend. A boy from the school."

"Ah, yes, I was wondering if he'd turn up." For the first time since taking the call from Sir Lionel, Angus Quilch—the Tiger—allowed himself a small smile.

28

There was silence in Ardman's office. Sir Lionel sat with his head in his hands. Eventually, he looked up, face pale and voice strained as he said: "I've made a terrible error of judgment."

"He took us all in," Ardman said.

"That is not an excuse. And he was my *friend*. Or so I thought."

"We've all been guilty of misjudgment," Chance said.

"I shall resign at once." Sir Lionel got to his feet. "I'll make an appointment to see Henderson in the prime minister's office as soon as I can."

"No," Ardman said sternly. "I'd rather you did nothing for the moment, Sir Lionel. The last thing we need now is a change of command."

"What *do* you want?" Sir Lionel asked quietly.

"The authority to pursue this. To do whatever it takes to get back the Banker and Rich Chance and expose the Tiger."

"You have it."

"I'll need it in writing," Ardman said.

"Of course. Anything else?"

"Go home," Ardman said. His voice was devoid of emotion—no accusation, but no sympathy either. "I think it best if you keep out of the way and let my people do their job."

He did not wait for Sir Lionel's reply but turned at once to Chance. "Get up there, John. Quickest way possible. I'm afraid our ruse may have backfired—the Tiger believes he only has until nine tomorrow morning. We may have forced him into taking extreme action." He sighed. "I'm sorry. Do what you can until Goddard gets a full assault team in place."

Sir Lionel slipped out of the room, his shoulders bowed and his head down.

"I'll get on to the RAF," Chance was saying. "There's an air base just thirty miles from Calder. I expect they can find me a car."

"I expect they'd appreciate it back in one piece," Ardman said. He turned to Goddard. "Best option?"

"It's a castle on an island and they may be expecting trouble," Goddard said. "We know they have small arms and grenades. We could do with some heavy-duty backup just to be on the safe side."

"SAS, then," said Chance.

"We'd need the full backing of COBRA before they could go in," Goddard pointed out.

"You'll have it," Ardman assured him. "Get on to the SAS at Hereford. Get them briefed and up there soonest."

Chance was already on his cell phone. "I want a car ready

and a personal call to Air Vice Marshal Remick at CHQ, and I want them in the next five minutes."

A narrow road skirted a stretch of woodland that extended to the coast. It was the closest they could get by car. From the map, it looked like an easy walk through the woods. Then Jade and Halford would find themselves opposite the island of Calder.

Halford drove the rental car off the road, leaving it on a stretch of grass between road and wood. They hadn't seen another vehicle for over an hour. As soon as Jade got out of the car, she realized the walk was not going to be as straightforward as she had hoped. Her foot sank into the mud, and she saw that the car had left deep tracks where it had pulled onto the grass.

"Will we get it out of the mud again?" she wondered.

"Let's worry about that when we need to," said Halford. "Brought your boots?"

They trudged across the grass and into the woods. The ground was not so damp there, sheltered under the trees. It was almost dark, but Halford had thought to buy two powerful Maglites at an electronics shop at Heathrow. Not only were they powerful, he had told Jade, but virtually indestructible too.

The woods seemed to go on forever, and Jade hoped Halford knew where he was going. She guessed the man had a good sense of direction from his army days. How often must he have traipsed across desert or through jungle behind enemy lines?

There seemed to be a vague path through the trees—a natural way to go where the trees were slightly wider apart and the ground a little worn away. Was it accidental? Jade wondered.

She listened but could hear no signs of life apart from their own footsteps crunching through dead wood and sloughing through leaves. Beyond that she thought she could hear the sound of the sea—waves breaking on the rocky shore. She was still looking around and listening intently when Halford stopped suddenly. So suddenly that Jade almost walked into him.

"What is it?"

"Not sure," Halford said. He was shining the light at a patch of ground just ahead of them.

Damp leaves had blown across, forming a small pile. But Jade could see the glint of metal as well. Someone had deliberately hidden something under the leaves, right in the middle of the path—just where anyone would naturally walk to get to the coast.

"It's a trap," she realized. Both Jade and Halford froze, not daring to move. "We're in a minefield."

The RAF Tornado F3 Air Defense Variant was flying with its wings swept back. It usually had a crew of two, but on this flight the pilot was taking a passenger—John Chance.

Chance was wearing one of the new skintight LARM flight suits that were still on the secret list. It was similar to a standard flight suit, with liquid held between two layers of tough material. Chance was surprised to find it didn't hamper his movements at all.

The liquid was as thin as water, barely more than a millimeter thick. But as well as maintaining his body warmth while flying at twelve thousand meters, it reacted to pressure. He had felt it molding into shape under the weight of his body as he squeezed into the Tornado cockpit. That was why it was called liquid armor. If the pilot ejected or was in a crash, the suit would become a protective shell wherever there was an impact. And provided it wasn't fired from too close and wasn't an armor-piercing round, the liquid could also harden quickly and solidly enough to stop a bullet.

"Got you a car, sir." The pilot's voice was filtered and distorted but clear enough.

"Thanks."

"Base commander's lending you his. Says to tell you he's been warned to ask for it back in one piece."

"Not a problem," Chance assured him. "Well, probably not," he added quietly.

"And if you get a chance, it could do with a wash."

"I think I might be pressed for time. How are we doing?"

"Not long now, sir. Just touching Mach two point three. Pretty much top speed."

"And what's that in English for us non-techies?" Chance wondered. He knew it was fast. He could feel himself being pressed into the seat and the suit reacting whenever the aircraft banked or turned.

"It's about fifteen hundred miles per hour." The pilot turned slightly, though his face was all but hidden behind his flight mask. "Beats the train any day."

Keeping the flashlight steady on the pile of leaves, Jade watched as Halford carefully removed one leaf at a time.

"You were right," he said at last. "It is a trap. But not quite as sophisticated as we thought."

He moved aside so that Jade could see what he had uncovered. Two small arcs of metal with sharp teeth cut into them were held apart by a sprung baseplate. An animal trap.

"That's so cruel," Jade exclaimed.

"It wasn't meant for us. Too small. Hoping to catch a hare, maybe."

He picked up a stick and poked it at the trap. The two sprung jaws snapped together and the dry stick shattered. Jade winced.

"Who would set a thing like that?" Jade demanded. "That's got to be illegal."

"I'm guessing this is private land too," Halford said. "So he's probably a poacher."

"Who?" Jade asked.

"The man who thinks I can't hear him as he sneaks up on us from behind you," a voice called out.

Jade whirled around in time to see a dark figure step out from among the trees.

"So you're not as clueless as I thought," the man said in

a thick Scottish accent. "Heard you from about a mile away crashing through the woods here. I wondered if you'd maybe find my traps."

"They're horrible," Jade told him. "You should be ashamed of yourself."

"Oh, for catching wee animals? Don't worry, lass—the rabbits I miss will be torn apart by the local foxes. Might take them longer to die, of course, but hey—that's Mother Nature for you."

"You're a very sick man, you know that?"

"And you're trespassing here as much as I am," the poacher pointed out. Now that he was closer, Jade could see he was in late middle age—a small man with gray stubble around his slack chin. "What you doing? Not after a rabbit for the pot, that's for sure."

"We're looking for Calder Island, for the castle," Halford said. "Maybe you can help us?"

"And why should I do that?"

"We'd be very grateful," Halford said.

The poacher pointed the way they'd been heading. "Keep going the way you are, you'll reach the sea. You can't miss the island."

"Is it easy to get to? The island?" Jade asked.

The poacher laughed. "Impossible. Unless you're hiding a boat somewhere. Got one in your pocket, maybe? Inflatable, is it?"

"Too far to swim?" Halford asked.

"Unless you've swum the Channel, I'd say so. Oh, it isn't too far, but the sea's not kind and it's mighty cold. You'd freeze to death before you drown, I'm thinking. There's the old causeway, but that's underwater now. Some say you can walk across at low tide, but I wouldn't want to try it. Even if you knew the route, I'd think it's crumbled and rotted away by now. You'd be over your head before you got halfway."

"We need to go back for a boat," said Jade.

"You're serious, aren't you?" the poacher said in surprise. "You really want to get across to the island?"

"Yes, actually, we do," Jade said.

"Like I said, we'd be grateful for any help or advice," Halford said. He pulled his wallet from his pocket and held it where the poacher could see. "Extremely grateful."

"Can you help?" Jade asked.

The poacher sniffed. "Depends on how you feel about fishing. Know how you feel about rabbiting. What about fish? Catching them in a net cruel too, is it?"

Jade opened her mouth to tell him that yes, it was, actually. But Halford put a hand on her shoulder to stop her.

"You a fisherman as well?" he asked.

"Might be."

"With your own boat?"

"Might have."

"Which could be for hire?"

"Might be."

Jade sighed. "Oh, for God's sake, give him some money and let's get this boat."

The boat didn't look very safe. It was an old wooden rowboat with water sloshing about in the bottom. The paint on the outside was chipped and cracked, and the varnish inside was flaking off like cellophane. One of the oars had a chunk taken out of it as if it had been bitten by a shark. Jade hoped it hadn't.

The poacher had his boat tied up to a large rock in an inlet out of sight of the island. The island with its huge castle was a dark shape in the distance, looming up against the dark gray of the sky. There were dim lights at some of the windows, and Jade thought she could see a curl of black smoke rising from it. The whole place looked dark, oppressive and forbidding.

The poacher took a bundle of ten-pound notes from Halford and left them to it. He disappeared almost silently back into the woods.

"Are we really going over there in this thing?" Jade asked.

"No," Halford told her. "At least—you're not."

"What?"

"Your father told me to look after you and not let you get into trouble. Going over there is trouble with a capital *T*."

"But Rich is over there."

"*Probably* over there," he corrected her. "I'll go alone. And I'll find out for sure. If he is, maybe I can get him out. More likely, I'll have to come back or send you a signal. But once we know for sure, then we can sit tight and wait for Ardman."

"Oh, great. So why bother coming at all? Why not just sit tight back in London till Ardman gets his finger out?"

"Because," Halford told her, "if Rich is there, then he's in trouble and needs help. And fast."

"Then let's go." Jade put one foot into the boat. It rocked precariously under her weight.

Halford pulled her back out. "I'm serious, Jade. You're not coming. That boat won't take both of us safely. Let's face it, it probably won't take one of us safely."

"I'm lighter than you," Jade protested. "I'll go."

Halford laughed. "No, you won't. Anyway, I've got a wooden leg, so I'll float."

"That's crazy and it isn't wood, it's plastic or something. I've seen it." But Jade laughed despite herself.

"You call your dad and tell him what's going on. If I know John Chance, he's on his way up here already—whatever Ardman says."

"Okay," Jade said. "I'll call Dad." The wind was pulling at her coat and she pulled it tight around her. "But you—be careful. And get Rich out safely."

"Right." He untied the boat.

"And be quick."

"Quick as I can," Halford promised.

He climbed down into the boat and pushed it away from the shore with one of the oars. Jade watched him start rowing toward the island with practiced ease.

She couldn't get a signal on her cell phone. Typical. But maybe it would be better from higher up—back in the woods. Still cursing Halford under her breath, Jade knew in her heart that he was right. She retraced her steps slowly, watching the display on her phone, waiting for any tiny suggestion of a connection.

She heard the voice at the same moment the phone got a signal. Jade froze. Listened. Looked around.

There was a faint glow from between the trees, a ways off to the left. Slowly and silently, she edged toward it, struggling to hear. She recognized the poacher's accent before she could make out his words. The glow was his own cell phone. But who was he calling?

"That's right, two of them. Man and a girl . . ."

Jade stopped dead.

The poacher listened, then went on. "Oh, I tried to put them off, but the mad jokers were desperate to get to your castle. So I lent them my boat. Figured you'd take care of them better than me. Figured you'd be grateful too. As usual."

Jade backed slowly away. The poacher ended his call and moved off deeper into the woods. As soon as she felt safe, Jade turned and ran. She called Halford on her cell phone, hoping the signal would hold. But all she got was his voice mail—her cell phone might be connecting, but his wasn't.

By the time she got back to the inlet, she could see no sign of the little boat. Halford was heading into a trap, and there was no way Jade could warn him.

29

Rich and the Banker had talked for a long time. There didn't seem to be any way out of it. If they didn't give the Tiger the information he wanted, he would kill them. But the Banker said he didn't know it—the data was written down, and his daughter had that safe. His daughter, who could be dead for all he knew. Rich didn't press the man on the subject.

And in any case, it seemed to Rich that if they did somehow get the information the Tiger wanted, he would kill them once he had it. A lose-lose scenario.

"Even if Eleri is all right," the Banker said sadly, "she must be in Mr. Ardman's care. He isn't likely to allow her to get the access codes and account numbers to us."

"Let's just hope she's got them safe," Rich said glumly.

"Oh, quite safe," the Banker said. "You see, we had the information etched with a laser—"

He broke off as the door suddenly opened. The Tiger stepped into the room. From his demeanor and bearing, Rich knew at once it was him.

"You're early," Rich said.

"Such wit," the Tiger replied. "I can see that we're in for a treat tomorrow." He turned to go, then paused. "I knew there was something." He turned back, his face split by an unpleasant smile. "I just had a telephone call from a local gentleman who has my interests at heart. I thought I would pass on the message."

"And what's that?" Rich asked. It didn't look from the Tiger's smile as if it would be good news.

"Well, I don't know if you are aware that at this very moment, a couple of your friends are attempting a daring and dramatic rescue. With a boat and everything."

Rich looked at the Banker—could it be true?

"A man and a girl," the Tiger went on. "So very sad. I just wanted to tell you that I'm afraid the rescue is . . ." He paused, licking his lips as he savored the moment. ". . . And I think this phrase is particularly apt. Dead in the water."

With a sudden guffaw of laughter at his own joke, the Tiger turned to leave. But then he paused and turned back.

"Bannock—there are no windows in this room."

"No, sir."

"That's not good at all. Please see that my guests are moved to a more-convenient room. One that has a good view of where our infrared cameras have picked up the boat. I'd hate for them to miss the show."

Chance had managed to squeeze a small bag of clothes and equipment into the cockpit with him. He quickly pulled on dark trousers and a sweater and jacket over the top of his LARM flight suit.

He tossed the bag onto the passenger seat of the performance blue Ford Focus ST. It was parked at the side of the service road, close to the runway where the Tornado had come to a stop. Beside it was an illuminated sign warning that the speed limit on the base was twenty miles per hour. Chance assumed that applied to the roads, not the runways.

"You will take care of it?" Wing Commander "Flip" Anderson asked anxiously.

"Like it was my own," Chance assured him, climbing in.

Anderson didn't look much encouraged. "I've only had it a month. It's got nearly as many gadgets and controls as the Tornado. I'm still working some of them out."

"Which one's the ejector seat?" Chance asked with a grin.

The joke seemed to make Anderson more anxious. "You sure it'll be all right?"

"I'm only driving thirty miles to the coast." Chance adjusted the position of the seat and the rearview mirror. "What could possibly happen?"

"Well . . ." But Anderson's comment was lost in the guttural sound of the engine. The car reached sixty miles per hour before it got to the gates.

Chance had pulled up a map of the area around Calder in the plane and memorized the useful details. There was a small wood on the coast closest to the castle. But if he drove past that, the road doubled back after ten miles and then came out at a point on the seafront farther along. It was a greater distance across to the castle, but it was probably a good place from which to assess what was going on, and he'd have the car with him ready for a quick getaway or a rendezvous elsewhere. For the moment, Chance was on his own. But he was expecting Ardman to arrange company for him very soon.

He got company quicker than he expected.

Twenty minutes after leaving the RAF base, Chance was passing the wood he had seen on the map. He thought he caught a glimpse of another car in the black of the night, parked off the edge of the road, almost in the trees. But as he glanced over, he saw something else, farther ahead.

A figure stepped out of the trees and walked into the road—right in the path of the car.

Chance slammed on the brakes. The antilock light flashed on as he tried to steer away from the man. Everything seemed to happen in slow motion, and Chance could make out every detail of the figure picked out in the brilliant glare of the headlights as he stood motionless in the road.

The man was wearing a long dark coat that flapped in the wind, revealing a dark suit beneath. Despite the fact that it was pitch black apart from Chance's headlights, he was wearing dark glasses.

But Chance had judged it perfectly. The car screeched to a halt less than a meter short of the man, who nodded appreciatively.

Chance was already pulling his handgun from the bag on the passenger seat. He tucked it into the back of his trousers out of sight, then got out of the car. "What the hell do you think you're doing?" he yelled at the man.

The man smiled back and took off his glasses. "I'm pleased to see you too, my friend. Any chance of a lift?"

Chance stared in disbelief. "Ralph? But—how did you know it was me?"

Ralph shrugged. "Who else would be driving like a maniac along this road in the middle of the night?" He opened the passenger door. "You mind if I move your bag?"

The room was right at the top of one of the towers. The roof of the tower had been glassed in like a conservatory, except the glass was a geodesic dome of angled panels. There was a small metal telescope set up on a bracket at one side, facing in the direction of the mainland. Not that Rich could see the mainland. In fact, he could see hardly anything, the night was so dark.

Bannock had pushed Rich and the Banker out of the stone staircase that emerged into the room and then pulled the heavy wooden door closed behind them. The sound of his laughter was cut off by the slam of the door.

"I don't know what he thinks we'll be able to see from up here," the Banker said.

The place was lit by small but powerful lamps set into the stone floor. The light cast eerie shadows across the glass dome. Rich walked quickly to the telescope. Maybe it was infrared. But through it he could see almost nothing. A dark mass that might be the mainland, but no sign of a boat. Or of Jade.

"Whatever he's planning," Rich said, "it'll be something we can see. He'll have light when he wants it. But Jade and Dad—or whoever it is—they don't know they're heading into a trap."

"And we can't warn them. Not from up here."

Rich wasn't so sure. "If we had a flashlight, we could shine a warning."

"But shine it where?" the Banker asked.

"All around. Up here we could make this tower into a sort of lighthouse."

"Except," the Banker pointed out, "we don't have a light."

Rich knelt down beside one of the lamps in the floor. It was protected by a thick glass cover, but there was a slightly raised metal rim. "If I can pry this open, we can get the lamp from inside."

"I doubt it will come out."

"We won't know unless we try, will we?" Rich said.

He could feel his nails tearing as he scrabbled to get them under the metal rim. It was a slow and frustrating process, but Rich thought he could feel the thing moving. Soon he was sure, and the warm metal rim and the glass cover came away in his hand.

The Banker joined him and shielded his eyes from the glare of the lamp. The glass had been slightly tinted, so beneath the cover the light was even brighter. It was hot too. Rich could feel the heat as he reached for the bulb and snatched his hand away.

"The bulb on its own isn't much use," the Banker pointed out.

"Have you got a hanky or something I can use as a glove?" Rich was already wrapping his own hanky around his fingers. Would it be enough to stop him from getting burned? "It looks like the bulb is just connected to a wire. There may be some slack in it."

The Banker handed Rich his hanky. "You could be right. Let's pray you are . . ."

Rich managed to lift the bulb and its connector out of the housing and onto the stone floor. But the wire was only about a meter long. "We can't lift it high enough." He looked around. "I doubt if any of the others are much different, even if we had time to get at them all and see."

Lights came on in the castle courtyard below. They could see through the dome that Bannock and a group of other men were walking quickly across the castle and climbing the battlements farther along. In the dim light from the courtyard, Rich could see them setting up searchlights. And something that looked like a gun.

"We could try shining the light through the telescope if it comes free," the Banker suggested. "Though that will only shine it upward."

Rich ran to the telescope. It was fixed to a tilting bracket, but the fastenings were badly rusted, and Rich guessed it had been there for longer than the glass dome. The damp, salty sea air had done them a favor, and a good tug from Rich got the telescope free of the bracket. The Banker was right: clamping the telescope over the light shone a focused beam upward. Rich put his hand over it.

"We need something to angle it down again," the Banker said.

"Your glasses?"

They tried, but the thick pebble lenses only diffused the light. Rich tried angling the tinted glass cover he had pulled free, but that did no good either—the light just shone through it.

"We need something like a prism," the Banker said. "Perhaps if we smashed the dome, we might get a piece of angled glass."

"A prism! Of course." Rich rummaged frantically in his pockets. "Don't say I've lost it."

"Lost what?"

"This!" Rich pulled the large diamond triumphantly from his pocket.

The Banker's mouth dropped open in astonishment.

"I got it from Eleri," Rich explained. He held it over the light shining up through the telescope. The diamond seemed to glow from within, but by angling it, he managed to catch a facet that deflected the light.

"Do you know what that is?" the Banker asked quietly.

"It's a great big diamond—a huge prism."

Rich stared into the heart of the stone, marveling at the way the light reflected around within it. It was almost blue, it was so intense. And right in the heart of the diamond . . . Rich peered closer. "There's something inside. Very small. Tiny. Looks like writing or something. An imperfection?"

"It is not an imperfection," the Banker said. "It is a set of numbers. Account numbers and access codes."

Rich looked at the Banker, the reflected light playing across the man's face and shining off his glasses. "This is where the data is stored?"

"All the information that the Tiger needs. And you had it here all the time. If he finds out—he'll take the diamond. He'll have the money. And he will kill both of us as well as your friends out there."

"The road forks just up ahead," Ralph said. "You want to go right."

"I know," Chance told him.

"And I really think you should slow down. You could seriously injure someone."

"I'm getting close to it," Chance admitted. "Now, what are you doing here?"

"I'm afraid I lied to you in Venice. My Italian colleagues actually stand to lose an awful lot of money if the Banker hands over the account details. Whether he gives them to you or to the Tiger, they still lose out. So, it was time to call in a favor. They knew that I had certain friends in British intelligence, and Scevola made it very clear to me what would happen if I didn't make contact on his behalf. He really isn't a very nice man, you know. Just here," he added as they reached the fork in the road.

"You want me to get Ardman to let you keep your money?" Chance slowed very slightly for the turn. "I can't do that."

"That's a pity," Ralph said. "A great pity."

They drove in silence for almost a minute. Then Ralph went on, "You know, I don't mind so much if Ardman and your people get the money. Financially speaking, I don't stand to lose very much at all. But if the Tiger gets it, he will be even richer than he was before. He will be in a position to challenge our business ventures—mine and Signor Scevola's."

"Can't have that," Chance replied. "Tell you what—you leave the Tiger to me. Can I drop you somewhere?"

"I knew you'd see sense, my friend. There is one *slight* complication in that Scevola has made it very plain that if I don't persuade you to get his money back, he will kill me." Ralph grinned suddenly. "But you can leave me to worry about that. You can drop me just before we reach the coast. There is a turnoff that will do. We'll be there in . . ." He made a point of looking at his watch. "Oh, I knew there was something—sorry, I so nearly forgot."

"Forgot what?"

"About the watch."

"What watch?"

"The one I gave Rich. I'm afraid it contains an extra feature."

Chance felt himself go cold. "What feature?"

"A small but immensely powerful explosive capsule. Like I said—time to call in the favors. You do a little favor for me, like get my account numbers and pass codes so that Scevola doesn't have me shot. In return, I shall do a little favor for you. Like make sure that explosive capsule isn't triggered by a remote signal from Signor Scevola. Because if it is, Rich will never know the time again."

The car stopped almost as abruptly as it had when Ralph first stepped in front of it.

Chance turned slowly to face his passenger. "You do anything to harm Rich and I'll kill you."

Ralph smiled sadly. "I know. So for both our sakes, let us hope you can get me what I want."

"Why can't you get it? You found the Tiger."

"Hardly. I have no idea who the Tiger is and until very recently no idea where he was. I assume it is the Tiger you are coming to see, but I confess I might be wrong. I was merely waiting for you."

"And how did you know where I would be?"

"A lucky guess," Ralph confessed. He waited while Chance started the car moving again, then continued. "It seemed likely that you would come after Jade when she made a sudden trip up here."

"You've been watching Jade?"

Ralph laughed. "Not exactly. There is a tracking device inside one of the glass beads on that lovely necklace I gave her."

The dark shape of the castle was looming large above Halford when he checked over his shoulder. His arms were aching from the effort of rowing, but it looked like it wasn't far now. If he had to, he would row right around the little island until he found somewhere to land the boat.

The good thing was that he had managed to get there without being seen. There didn't appear to be any security to speak of. He had caught an odd glimpse of movement on the battlements but nothing to worry about.

Until he saw the light.

It blinked out from the top of one of the towers. Three rapid bursts of brilliant white, shining across the water. Then a pause before three longer flashes. Then three short ones again. Several thoughts went through Halford's mind very rapidly. First, that the flashes represented SOS in Morse code. Second, that someone was therefore in trouble.

The last thing Halford had time to realize was that the someone in trouble was himself.

Then powerful searchlights cut through the night, picking out the small boat and dazzling Halford. He threw up his hands to shadow his eyes as the machine-gun fire started. Water splashed up all around. Splinters of wood whipped at his hands and face as holes drilled across the boat toward him.

On the shore, Jade felt her whole body heave with fear and horror as the tiny, distant boat tipped over. A moment later, she saw a trail of fire from the battlements of the castle.

A missile of some kind crashed into the middle of the pool of light, disappearing under the broken boat. A moment later the water erupted in a violent explosion as the sea itself seemed to catch fire.

Smoke drifted across the area of light. Behind it, Jade could see only the splintered debris from the rowboat.

30

The old poacher was standing in the woods, close to where Jade had last seen him. There was a gap through the trees and he was staring down at the sea—watching the wreckage of the little rowboat still burning where the rocket-powered grenade had exploded.

"That was my boat," he said to Jade as she approached. He sounded shocked; his eyes were wide and his face was pale when Jade turned her Maglite full on him.

"That was my friend," Jade said. "And you told them he was coming."

The poacher shook his head, his mouth still hanging open. "My boat. I—I didn't know they'd do that. I thought they'd pay me a few quid and see him off the premises. They have before."

"Yeah, well, now you know the sort of people we're dealing with," Jade said angrily. She was in shock herself, she realized—shaking uncontrollably. If she stopped talking, her teeth would start chattering. "They're crazy murderers, and they've got my brother and another man prisoner over there. You're going to help me get them out."

"Not me." He backed away, evidently terrified by what he'd seen. "I ain't doing nothing."

"You're helping me," Jade insisted, advancing toward him with the Maglite held like a club. "Whether you like it or not."

"You're mad." The poacher stopped as he reached a tree and pressed against it, cowering from Jade. "I haven't got another boat."

"Reckon I'm mad now? Wait till you see me when I get to the island. Think I'm mad? Wait till you hear how I'm going to get there."

"There's no way. Not now my boat's gone."

"You said there was a causeway—that it used to be passable till the sea rose or the road sank or whatever."

"I said no one's been across in years."

"At low tide, it's passable," Jade reminded him.

"*May* be passable. And low tide isn't for . . ." He risked a quick look at his watch. "Not for another hour."

"Long enough for me to get started and hope the water doesn't get too deep before I get too far. And if I can't get across, I'll come back—I'll come back and I'll find you."

"You are mad!" the poacher said. If anything, he'd gone even paler.

"And while I'm trying not to drown and to rescue Rich, you're going for help. You're going to the police . . ."

"Police?" It was almost a yelp.

"The police, and you're going to tell them that someone blew up your boat and the man you lent it to. Tell them to get in touch with a man called Ardman—they can find him through MI5, I should think."

"MI5?" The poacher almost collapsed as his legs gave way.

Jade grabbed him and hauled him up against the tree. She had the flashlight pressed across his throat. "Ardman, MI5—remember that. You tell them what happened and make sure they send help or—I mean it—I'll be back for you."

"But—the police, my traps . . ."

"I don't care about your traps. You've got a cell phone—call for help. Then clear them away before the cops get here. But first, before anything else, show me where this causeway is."

Jade had stopped shaking and worked off a lot of her anger and emotion. With some satisfaction—and the distant hope that maybe Halford had survived somehow—she followed the poacher through the woods to where he said the causeway used to be.

Shining her light at the ground, she could make out what might once have been a cobblestone roadway, covered at the edge with grass and earth. It led into the woods in the direction of the pathway that she and Halford had followed—perhaps it had originally been the road over to the castle.

A few minutes later, with the poacher long gone, Jade was having second thoughts. Would he really call the police? Should she have done it herself and risked having to wait in the woods where she could get a signal while being transferred from department to department for ages? She'd gambled it was better to get across to the island as quickly as possible.

Now the water was up to her waist; her legs were almost completely numb. The castle was a black cutout against the sky that seemed as far away as ever. And the water was getting deeper and colder with every step.

As Rich had expected, the Tiger came to gloat. But Rich and the Banker were ready.

Rich stood near the door where the stairs emerged, hands behind his back. The Banker was a short way away, directly in front of the door. His hands were also behind his back. They had heard the sound of feet on the stairs, and Rich just hoped the Banker could hold on to the hot lamp for long enough. He had his hands wrapped in handkerchiefs, but even so, it must be burning his fingers.

Rich's school blazer was in tatters. He had ripped the sleeves off and managed to tear the rest of it down the middle. That gave him four pieces of dark material, which he had used to cover four of the lamps set in the floor—the four closest to the stairs. They were so bright that light still filtered through the material, and there were several lights they hadn't managed to cover. But overall, the light in the room was reduced to a dim twilight.

The door was unlocked and opened at last. The Tiger stepped into the glassed-in room, Bannock close behind him.

Rich was relieved to see there was no one else with them and Bannock was not holding a gun. He evidently didn't think a boy and a nervous little man posed any threat.

He was about to find out he was wrong.

"I trust you enjoyed the show," the Tiger said. He didn't seem to have noticed how dark it was, his mind obviously on other things. "Sadly, there will be no encore." He walked toward the Banker. "And now that you have seen what I am willing to do, I think it's time to give me what I want."

"I think he's right," Rich said loudly. He saw both Bannock and the Tiger relax slightly at his words—they thought they had won. "Let him have it."

The Banker brought his hands from behind his back—holding the light Rich had freed from the floor. He shone it directly at the Tiger and Bannock. With the other light reduced, it was even brighter—even more dazzling. The Tiger threw his arms up in front of his face with a cry. Bannock staggered back, blinking, his hand reaching into his jacket.

Bringing the heavy metal telescope from behind his back and careful not to look at the light the Banker was holding, Rich stepped quickly up to Bannock and swung the telescope like a club. It whumped into the man's stomach, and he doubled over. The next blow came down on the man's exposed neck, and he slumped to the floor.

The Tiger had turned. He too was blinking, unable to make out what was going on. "Bannock?!" he yelled.

"Come any closer and I'll brain you!" Rich warned.

The Tiger realized what had happened to his henchman and

didn't move. The Banker dropped the light and ran quickly to join Rich. Together they backed away, out the door and onto the small landing outside.

"You won't get away with this," the Tiger told them angrily.

"Watch us," Rich said. He pulled the door shut and locked it. Almost immediately, there was a hammering from the other side. But it was muted and muffled by the thick wood. Rich took the heavy, old-fashioned key out of the lock and stuffed it in his pocket.

"What now?" the Banker asked as they hurried down the stairs.

"We need to find somewhere to hide. It won't be long before they're missed and someone goes looking for them."

"But they can't get out for a while," the Banker said.

Rich wasn't sure if it was a question, whether he wanted reassurance that they were safe for the moment. But before he could answer, they heard the sound of a gunshot and the splinter of wood.

"Should have taken Bannock's gun," he realized. "They're shooting out the lock or the hinges."

"We can't get out of the castle—where can we go?" the Banker demanded, panicking. "Where can we hide?"

"In the last place they'll look for us," Rich told him.

There was another shot from above them. It seemed louder, echoing down the stone staircase.

Floodlights came on, illuminating the castle on its island. Until then, Chance had been unable to see it. He had stared out over the dark expanse of water but could make out nothing in the moonless night.

"Thoughtful of them," Ralph remarked. "I wonder why they have done that."

"Maybe someone's causing them some trouble and they want to see what's going on," Chance suggested. "I can think of a couple of candidates. Actually, three," he added as he remembered that Dex Halford was with Jade.

"Might make your job a little easier. Remember, you have until dawn. After that . . ." Ralph clapped his hands together, miming an explosion.

"Thank you," Chance muttered.

"No problem. And you can drop me just along here, if you wouldn't mind."

There was a large black limousine parked in a small turnoff at the side of the narrow lane. Chance brought the Focus to a halt beside it. He could see the skull-like silhouette of a man sitting in the backseat. Scevola.

"Don't get any ideas," Ralph said quietly. "Scevola is a dedicated and ruthless man. He cares for nothing but money, I'm afraid. He doesn't like me very much, when all is said and done. So, if it were up to me . . ." He shrugged. "Do what you can, my friend. And I will do what I can. That's all I can offer."

Chance turned to look the man in the eyes. "It had better be enough. Because if not, if anything happens to Rich, then I'll be after you. After you both."

Ralph smiled back grimly. "Then I wish you good luck. If the Tiger gets the money, I can do nothing to help. If you get the money and the Tiger is denied it, then there is a possibility I can persuade Scevola that things are not so bad." He offered his hand.

Chance did not take it. "Tell me something before you go."

"Anything."

"You gave Jade a necklace with a tracker in it."

"Indeed, I did."

"You gave Rich a watch with a bomb in it."

"Sorry."

"And you gave me a hip flask."

"You have it with you?"

"No. But tell me—what's its secret? Is it booby-trapped like the watch? Or trackable? Or filled with a slow-acting poison? Or what?"

Ralph opened the car door. "It's a flask," he said. He sounded hurt. "Just a flask, nothing more. It's a present, from one friend to another. I thought you would like it, and you don't even carry it with you." He climbed out of the car. "Some people are just so ungrateful." He shook his head sadly as he slammed the door behind him.

Chance didn't wait to see Ralph get into the limo. He put the Focus into gear and stamped down on the accelerator. Ahead of him the road was a dark ribbon snaking toward the floodlit castle in the sea.

• • •

The sea was so cold now that Jade couldn't feel it. She couldn't feel anything. She was treading water. When the causeway had dipped away too far for her to stand up any longer, she'd swum on—just for a few meters. Just to see if the causeway started to rise again as it approached the island.

It didn't. At least, not yet. And in the utter darkness, Jade had no idea where she was. She'd strayed from the path, and when she tried to put her feet down, there was no sign of causeway. No way of knowing where it was or which way she should go.

Light washed suddenly across the water as the castle lit up. Jade gasped with relief—she could see it, could see where she was going.

But it didn't help her find the causeway. The island was too far away for her to swim, even if she could feel her arms and legs and persuade them to do anything more than thrash weakly in the water.

Broken, splintered wood bobbed across between Jade and the island—all that was left of Halford's boat. Halford himself must be at the bottom of the sea. And seeing the wreckage, Jade knew that it had all been for nothing. And that soon she would be joining him.

31

The Tiger strode into his office in a foul mood. Bannock followed, equally angry. The big man had yelled at the first guards he'd seen and cuffed one around the head. But it hadn't helped either of them feel any better.

"We still don't have the account numbers or the access codes," the Tiger announced to anyone within earshot. "That kid and the Banker are running around doing God knows what and causing all sorts of damage. I can't even get a sandwich because the kitchen got blown up. What sort of operation are you running here?" he yelled at Bannock.

Bannock looked away, saying nothing.

"Satellite linkup is nearly complete," a man said nervously. "You can start the transfers from here." He pointed to the laptop computer set up on the Tiger's desk.

"Except I have nothing to transfer." The Tiger shook his head. Then he gave the slightest hint of a smile. "Apart from the ministry's own accounts."

He opened a folder lying beside the laptop. "I got the numbers and codes from that fool Lionel's own computer. He has no idea about security—even asked me what he should use as his password. Yes, let's see." He ran his finger down a list of names and numbers. "Mr. Ardman's budget for the next eighteen months would be a good start."

"They'll see as soon as you move anything," Bannock said. "They'll close the accounts down faster than we can get at them."

"Not all of them. But you're right. We betray our hand and show we're into the system too soon and we'll get next to nothing. They'll cut the satellite link. Better to wait until the last possible moment and clear out what we can along with the Banker's accounts."

"If we ever get to them," Bannock grumbled.

"We'll get to them," the Tiger assured him. "We'll get to them because you're going to find the Banker and make him give us the data we need. We'll get to them because if you don't, I'll have you hunted down and slaughtered like the dog you are, Bannock. You got that?"

Bannock stared at the Tiger, his lip curling in fury.

"And when you do get the data," the Tiger went on, "I'll increase your cut to ten percent. At a conservative estimate that will be something like a hundred million. And that's not dollars. Pounds sterling." He smiled. "Stick or carrot, whichever gets you motivated. Take your pick."

Bannock's eyes narrowed. He licked his dry lips and nodded. Then he hurried to give his men their orders.

"Oh, and Bannock," the Tiger called after him. "I need the Banker alive and able to talk. I really don't care what happens to the boy."

The wooden board looked like it had been shattered by the gunfire and explosions at one end. It was the largest surviving bit of the boat that Jade had found, and she clung to it with numbed hands as she kicked out, heading for the island. Without the floodlights, she would never have found the wood to use as a float or known where the island was. Maybe, at last, her luck was turning.

Though it was too late for Halford.

Jade bit her lip, trying to stop her teeth from chattering and to hold back her tears as she watched the castle grow larger and closer . . .

Rich had crossed his fingers and tried not to think about the previous time he'd headed back to the "last place they'll think of looking." But he was confident that Bannock would not bother searching for the Banker in the room he was supposed to be locked up in.

Fairly confident. If only they could get to it.

Huddled in a corridor, they could hear the sounds of men running, of Bannock shouting. Even the occasional gunshot.

"They're trying to frighten us," the Banker said. He sounded like it was working.

"Or taking it out on the seagulls," said Rich.

He clutched the heavy metal telescope tight. He could probably find a more suitable weapon—they'd even passed a couple of crossed swords and a shield mounted on the corridor wall. But Rich had another use in mind for the telescope. He was going to take out the Tiger. He'd seen what had happened to the boat—and whether Jade or his dad had been in it or not, the Tiger was going to pay.

With a deep breath to boost his courage and renew his determination, Rich set off down the corridor. If they did run into Bannock or any of the guards—well, that would be their problem, not his.

Close to exhaustion, Jade heaved herself up onto the wooden dock. She barely had the strength to climb up the ladder. She staggered along the wooden boards toward the huge castle gates.

The next problem would be how to get inside. Just so long as no one had seen her arrive—if they had, then getting inside might not be the problem. But first she had to warm up. She could barely stand, she was shivering so much. She couldn't feel her hands, never mind her fingers.

Jade slumped down against the rough stone castle wall beside the wooden gates. As her breathing subsided slightly, she slowly became aware of a dark shape close by. Like Jade, it was out of the main glare of the floodlights that illuminated the castle. A figure—a man. Looming over her.

Jade only had time for a brief startled cry before a hand clamped over her mouth.

• • •

The door was shut and the key was in the lock. Rich locked the door behind them. If Bannock did think of looking for them back in the rooms where the Banker and Rich had been imprisoned earlier, then maybe the locked door would be enough to put him off. Or if not, Rich would get some warning they were trying to get in before they knocked down the door. And for what he had in mind, he would need a warning. He could not afford to let the Tiger or Bannock or anyone else see what he was doing.

There was a bright lamp on the desk, which would be useful. Rich found a pen in one of the desk drawers, and he had a piece of notepaper in his pocket along with the diamond. The hardest part was dismantling the telescope.

"What are you planning to do?" the Banker asked. "Write a letter of complaint? Maybe a message to go in an old whiskey bottle?" He seemed less nervous now that they were back in the familiar room with the door locked behind them.

Rich was feeling a sense of relief too. They were safe, at least for the moment, and he had a plan—of sorts. He explained it to the Banker.

"Insurance," the Banker said thoughtfully.

"It doesn't really solve anything," Rich admitted. "But it maybe gives us something to bargain with if we need it. If only I can get this telescope apart."

The metal was chipped and rusted—dented slightly where Rich had hit Bannock over the head. But there was a tiny screw holding the cap at one end in place. If he could get the screw undone, maybe the telescope would come apart.

"This any good?" The Banker held up a slim wooden letter opener from another of the desk drawers. "A bit blunt and flimsy to be any use as a weapon. But it might pry apart the telescope."

It took a while—longer than Rich would have liked. But eventually the telescope was in several pieces. The cylindrical metal housing and the lenses from either end were spread on the blotter on the desk. Rich turned on the lamp.

"Right," he said. "Now we're getting somewhere."

"Sorry," Halford said.

"What—for creeping up and grabbing me like that? You'd better be!" Jade said. "Good to see you, though."

They were huddled together in the shelter of the wall and out of the light. Both were shivering. Halford didn't seem as bad as Jade, who could barely talk.

"I got out of that boat as soon as they started shooting. The shock wave from the grenade almost knocked me out cold, though. And I mean cold." He chuckled. "But I did manage to get ashore. Even managed to keep my leg on; otherwise I'd be hopping to the rescue."

"I'm too cold for rescues," Jade admitted.

"We need to get coats or something or we'll catch our deaths out here."

"And be no help at all to Rich. If he's in there."

"He's in there," Halford said confidently. "I had a warning. Too late to be much use, but someone was trying to signal to me, I'm sure."

"Rich?"

"He's certainly resourceful enough."

"So what's the plan?"

"We get nice warm coats, then we get Rich and this Banker out of there."

"And where do we get coats?"

"Ask a couple of guards politely."

"And where do we find a couple of guards? We need to be inside that castle."

"Yes," Halford agreed. "I thought we'd knock on the door."

A dark red oblong shape was heading across the map on the LCD screen.

"Looks like a car," one of the two guards on duty said. "Heading this way."

"He'll have to stop at the cliff," the other guard pointed out.

"Wouldn't bet on it. Look at the speed he's going."

"Perhaps he'll swim for it."

"Freeze to death if he does. Not that we'd know. The infra-red won't pick up anything in the water—too cold for that."

"Probably just a joyrider or a boy racer. Better warn the boss, though."

"Yes," the first guard agreed. "You never know."

Once he reached the cliff a couple of miles ahead of him, Chance's options became rather limited. The road he was on turned to run along the coast close to the cliff edge. But how he was going to get from cliff to island was a problem he could worry about when he got there.

In less than two minutes.

Chance's face was a mask of grim determination.

Doing her best to look pathetic, Jade waited for an answer. She had knocked hard on the wooden gates to the castle. Now she was standing in front of a smaller door set into one of the main gates. She was cold and shivering, wet through, hair all over the place. Pathetic was about right.

The little door opened and a guard appeared. He was dressed in a dark uniform with a soft camouflage cap and had a rifle slung over his shoulder. He looked at Jade with surprise and suspicion.

"It's some girl," he called over his shoulder. "Scott—come and look at this."

"Never mind look at this," Jade told him. "I had an accident. Ended up in the water. Look at me—I need some help here."

A second guard joined the first. Both were grinning as they stepped through the doorway.

"We'll help you, love," the first guard said. "Need warming up, do you?"

"I could do with a coat," Jade said. "And one for my friend too."

The second guard—Scott—looked like he thought it was Christmas. "You got a friend?"

"Better believe it," Halford said, stepping out from the shadows beside the door.

"Oh, now, hang on," Scott started to say. But his words ended with a muffled yelp as Halford's fist connected with his jaw.

The first guard was struggling to pull the rifle off his shoulder. Jade thumped him hard, and he blinked with surprise more than pain.

"Give me your coat," Jade said, and punched him again.

The guard swayed, still fumbling for the gun, until Halford decked him. "So much for asking nicely," he said. "Come on—let's get the coats and then we're inside."

"So long as no one notices," Jade said. "We really need a diversion."

Just then, twin streaks of fire erupted from the castle battlements above them. Two missiles blazed through the sky, heading for the distant mainland.

"That'll do," Jade admitted. "I wonder what's going on."

The two missiles were brilliant orange against the night as they blazed toward the car. *So much for the element of surprise,* Chance thought. He waited until they were almost on him before wrenching the steering wheel abruptly to one side.

The car spun a full circle in the narrow road. The first missile hammered into the pavement twenty meters behind and debris rained down on the Focus. The windshield cracked across and a window exploded.

The second missile, a fraction behind the first, disappeared through the hedge at the side of the road. There was the low *crump* of detonation, and Chance felt the shock wave knock the car forward.

He turned it out of the spin and fishtailed down the road. There was another flash from the castle battlements—a third incoming missile. Then another. He couldn't hope to avoid them all.

The car accelerated down the road. The wind whipped noisily through the broken side window. The lines of flame behind the new missiles streaked toward Chance as he floored the accelerator.

When he reached the point where the road turned sharply to follow the line of the coast along the cliff tops, Chance held tight to the steering wheel—keeping the car on a straight-line course toward the island castle. The tires jolted up the curb and skidded through wet grass.

There was only the sound of the wind as the Focus hurtled over the edge of the cliff. As it fell, the missiles overshot it, slamming into the roadway above.

Chance braced himself, pressing back into the seat as the nose of the car dipped down and the dark water filled his vision. Then the whole vehicle punched into the sea. The cracked windshield collapsed and caved in. Freezing water poured through the side window and the hole where the windshield had been.

Suffocating darkness closed over Chance's head as the car sank.

32

The door of the room where Rich and the Banker were hiding exploded inward. Splinters of wood flew across the room, whipping at Rich's cheeks. The Banker was knocked off his feet by the blast.

Rich blinked and wiped his hand across his face. A figure stepped through the noise and the smoke. Rich backed away, but he collided with the Banker, who was stumbling back to his feet. They both fell to the floor, coughing and spluttering.

Bannock's bearded, angry face stared down at Rich and his hands closed tightly on the boy's throat. He dragged Rich to his feet and pushed him roughly from the room. Another man was dragging the Banker after them.

"No need to push," Rich said, picking himself off the ground.

Bannock grabbed him by the collar and pushed him onward, down the corridor.

"The Tiger's going to rip you to bits," he said. He grabbed

the Banker by the shoulder and pushed him roughly after Rich. "That's what Tigers do."

The loss of the windshield was a blessing. Chance was able to get out through the hole. He wrestled his way out of the car and kicked upward until, gasping, he broke the surface. His jacket was hampering his movement and he struggled out of it.

The Tiger and his men would expect whoever had been in the car to have drowned or to freeze in the water. At best, they might manage to get back to the shore—bruised and battered.

But the LARM suit had protected Chance from the worst effects of the impact, and now it kept his body as warm in the icy water as it had in the freezing cockpit of the Tornado. The castle looked to be a good ways off, but Chance was an excellent swimmer. He struck out swiftly, knowing that the life of at least one and possibly both of his children depended on him.

Two dark figures moved quickly across the castle courtyard, past the spider-like shape of the Tiger's helicopter. They wore dark uniforms and camouflage caps. One of them was limping slightly.

They watched helplessly as Rich and the Banker were led across the courtyard and in through another door. Then they emerged cautiously from the shadow of the helicopter.

"We have to get them away from here," Jade said.

"Yes, but how?"

"Follow them. Wait for an opportunity to help."

"If it ever comes," said Halford grimly. "But you're right. That's our best bet."

Jade pushed stray damp strands of her blond hair up into her cap. She and Halford each pulled the brims down as low as they dared.

"Guard duty?" Jade suggested.

"Guard duty," Halford agreed.

"We found this on him." To Rich's horror, Bannock was holding up the diamond.

"On the boy?" The Tiger took the diamond from Bannock and held it up to the light. "Quite beautiful. Exquisite. Though I suspect it is actually yours," he said, turning to the Banker.

The Banker did not reply.

"So, I ask myself—why do you have it?" the Tiger went on. "Valuable? Oh, undoubtedly. Insurance, perhaps. But then again, perhaps there is more to it than that . . ."

"What are you going to do to us?" Rich asked, hoping to distract the Tiger.

The Tiger continued to examine the diamond, turning it to catch the light. "I'm not going to do anything to you. I shall leave that to Bannock."

Rich felt cold as he saw the way the huge Scotsman grinned at the Tiger's words.

"Unless you tell me what I want to know," the Tiger went on. "And I warn you, time is running out. It will be dawn soon. I want to get my money transferred to rather safer accounts and then be away from here before any more of your friends come looking. It won't be long before Ardman finds me, I'm afraid."

"Why not just give up and go now?" the Banker asked. He sounded defiant, but Rich could see the little man was trembling.

"Oh, I'm sure there is no immediate rush. The advance party, if that was what it was, lost an argument with a couple of surface-to-surface missiles just now. You probably heard the noise. Sorry about that."

"You're mad," Rich blurted out. "Sick. A criminal. Why are you doing this?"

"Money. Everything comes down to money." The Tiger paused as his study door opened. But it was just two more of his guards in their black uniforms and camouflage caps.

"But how you get it, what you do with it is . . . wrong," Rich insisted.

The Tiger shrugged. "I am an investor. That's all. I lend money to enterprises that I think will turn a profit."

"Terrorists? Criminals? Rogue states?"

"Perhaps my remit is a little broader than most. But how is it any different from a man who invests in defense industries— in armaments? You know, most of the bullets and bombs that were used in the world last year were bought by U.S. taxpayers. You blame me for investing my own money in enterprises that I think will give a better return than NATO or Iraq or Afghanistan?"

"It's murder. Organized crime. People suffer," Rich protested.

The Tiger laughed. "You have no idea how this world really works, do you? What would you rather I invested in? Computer database systems for the health-care industry? Oh, good idea—that would be money right down the drain. I might as well give it away. Which is pretty much what our government does." He held the diamond in his fist and brandished it. "Have you any idea how much money I watched being wasted by the Home Office while I was working for dear Lionel? Any idea how it is frittered away and wasted when it could be invested in something that turns a profit?"

"It's not all about profit," the Banker said.

"Ah, the bank manager speaks. You've changed your tune. You were happy enough to take my money—anyone's money—and invest it wherever we told you."

"I was wrong," the Banker said simply. "And for your information, I was never happy. I never made that decision. It was just something that happened." He met the Tiger's gaze for a moment, then looked away. "I should have been brave enough to face up to that sooner. Should have stopped it at once."

"But instead, you took the money. Bought diamonds." The Tiger held the diamond between his thumb and index finger and stared into it. "Now, investing in beauty I *can* understand." He frowned, looked closer, then gestured urgently at Bannock. "Get me a magnifying glass. Quickly, man."

"A what?"

"Just do it!" the Tiger roared. "It's here, isn't it?" he said to the Banker, his eyes gleaming like the diamond. "The account data, everything—inside this diamond!"

Bannock turned to the Tiger's desk to look for a magnifying glass. The Tiger held the diamond up in triumph.

At that moment, one of the uniformed guards who had been standing by the door stepped quickly up to the Tiger and grabbed the diamond from him. Before the Tiger could react, the guard turned and punched one of the others full in the face before head-butting another. His cap came off.

"Dex?" Rich exclaimed.

"Run!" Halford told him.

The way to the door was clear. But Bannock—out of Halford's immediate reach—had drawn a pistol and was aiming at Halford. Rich hurled himself at the big man, knocking his arm as the gun went off.

The bullet thudded into the ceiling.

The Banker made a dash for the door, but the Tiger had recovered from his surprise and grabbed the little man's arm, wrenching him back.

Bannock threw Rich to one side, sending him crashing into the desk. Another guard—the only one that Halford hadn't attacked—reached down toward Rich.

His vision was blurred, and he blinked to try to clear it. Halford and Bannock were wrestling. Halford had hold of Bannock's gun hand. But the other guards were recovering and coming to help. The diamond fell to the floor as Halford tried desperately to keep the gun away. With a final effort, he pushed Bannock aside and limped rapidly for the door.

Bannock sprawled backward. One of the other guards was scrabbling for the diamond. Another guard ran after Halford. Rich lashed out, kicking the man's legs from under him. To his surprise, the guard pulling him to his feet made no effort to stop him.

The guard was slight of build and Rich turned, ready to wrench his arms away and thump hard at the man.

Except it wasn't a man.

The guard put a finger to her lips and winked. It was Jade.

"Get after him!" Bannock yelled at the other guards. They were already running from the room, one pausing to hand Bannock the diamond.

"Who is he? How did he get in here?" the Tiger demanded.

"No idea," Bannock growled. "But I'm going to find out before I kill him." He gave the diamond to the Tiger. "You really think this is it?"

"I'm sure of it. Now, where's that magnifying glass I asked you for?"

The two guards were not far behind him, and Halford knew there would soon be others. The first hints of dawn were streaking the sky, turning it from black to gray as he limped out of the castle and into the courtyard again.

They'd catch him soon. Or shoot him. He knew that. But

the important thing was that he was drawing the guards away from Rich and the Banker—allowing Jade a chance, just a possibility, of getting them away.

The guards at the main gate that Halford and Jade had knocked out had guns. If Halford could get that far, could get a gun, he could fight back and keep more of the Tiger's men occupied. He cursed himself under his breath for allowing Jade to talk him out of taking a gun in the first place.

"We're not shooting anyone," she'd said.

Which was a fine principle. But as the shouts and the first bullet followed Halford, it was a principle he felt happy to abandon in favor of survival.

Through the open part of the gates he could see the early light reflecting on the water. He limped onward, aware of the sound of running feet behind him. The shooting had stopped— they'd probably realized he was going nowhere.

Just as far as the guns outside the main gates.

But then a figure rose up out of the water, striding up the causeway, silhouetted against the sea. Heading inexorably toward Halford. He hesitated—friend or foe?

The figure reached the gates, glanced down at the fallen guards shivering and unconscious without their uniforms. He picked up one of the automatic rifles and pointed it directly at Halford.

"Down!" the figure yelled.

Halford dropped immediately to the ground, recognizing the voice and laughing out loud.

A burst of automatic fire drove the guards back. Halford

crawled to the nearest cover, an archway on the outer wall not far from the gates. A shadow fell over him, and he looked up to find that the figure from the sea was offering him the second guard's gun.

"Good to see you," Halford said, releasing the safety.

"Good to be seen," Chance told him. "Sorry to burst in on you like this, but some fool left the gate open."

"It will take a few minutes to set up the transfers," the Tiger's technical man said.

"It has to be done before nine o'clock," the Tiger insisted.

"That may not be the main problem," Bannock said as the renewed sound of gunfire came from outside. "Maybe we should get away from here. Make the transfers from somewhere safer."

"We'd never get the satellite link up again and hack into the banking system in time," the Tiger said. "Get out there and find out what's going on. We evacuate only if we have to. Set up the transfer," he told the technician. "I'll read you the account numbers and codes from the diamond when you're ready."

"We have to stop him," Rich whispered to Jade while everyone seemed occupied and Bannock was out of the room.

"How?" she murmured back.

He shrugged. "Just be ready."

The Tiger glared across at Rich. "What are you muttering about?"

Jade looked down so he couldn't see her face under the cap.

Rich shuffled and tried to look uncomfortable. "You should get out while you can," he said.

"Oh, thank you." The Tiger's lip curled. "When I want your advice, I'll beat it out of you."

Bannock ran back in. "There's just two of them. We have them pinned down near the main gates."

"Good. Well done, Bannock."

The phone on the Tiger's desk rang and he waved at Bannock to answer it. The big Scotsman listened for a moment, then put the phone down again.

"There's a boat coming," he said.

"Deal with it," the Tiger said calmly.

"What if it's Ardman's people?"

The Tiger's voice was hard. "I said deal with it."

33

The launch was big and powerful. It cut through the water, heading straight for the wooden dock by the causeway at the front of the castle.

"Friends of yours?" Halford shouted to Chance above the chatter of machine-gun fire.

"It's not Ardman," Chance yelled back. "He sent Goddard for the SAS. That's hardly their style."

As the boat got closer, Chance had a better view of the two men standing at the prow. They wore dark suits and dark glasses. One was slightly short, a little stocky. The other was tall and lean with a face like a skull.

"I think things are getting complicated," said Chance.

"You're telling me," Halford replied. "I'm out of ammunition."

From the battlements above, one of the guards fired on the boat. Bullets pinged off the deck and chipped the expensive paint.

Scevola did not flinch. He clicked his fingers and pointed at where the bullets had come from.

Another man in a suit and dark glasses rose into sight between Scevola and Ralph. He was holding a large, brutal-looking automatic rifle. The man barely took aim, firing from the hip. There was a cry from somewhere above Chance and a body tumbled from the battlements.

Bannock ran across the courtyard, taking advantage of the distraction to get past Halford and Chance. The body landed at his feet and he stared down at it, mouth open. Then he ran up the steps to the battlements and looked out to where the boat was now arriving at the dock.

Moments later, Bannock was running back the way he had come.

While the remaining guards looked out at the boat, unsure of what to do after Bannock's retreat, Chance ran across to Halford, throwing his rifle to him.

"Keep me covered," he called as he kept running after Bannock and into the castle.

"We have to get out of here," Bannock announced as soon as he was in the Tiger's study.

"What are you talking about?" the Tiger demanded. "We're almost ready to make the transfers."

"Forget it. That boat—"

"What about it? Who is in it?"

Bannock's face was pale behind the red beard. "It's Cesare Scevola."

242

The Tiger also paled. "We can do a deal. He just wants his money back.."

"Since when did Scevola only want his own money? I don't care what you're planning, but I'm getting out of here while I still can."

Jade was amazed to see the big man so obviously scared. It was all she could do to keep from grinning. She could see that Rich was smiling too.

Bannock turned to leave. He stepped out of the room.

"You coward!" the Tiger yelled after him.

Suddenly Bannock was back—flying backward into the study and landing in a crumpled heap on the floor.

John Chance stepped into the room, rubbing his knuckles. "I rather enjoyed that," he admitted. "Hello, Rich."

Chance saw Jade too, nodding slightly to show it but saying nothing.

From outside, the chatter of gunfire was now unrelenting. But it was getting louder—closer . . .

Bannock groaned and slowly got to his feet. His face was now as red and angry as his beard. He was holding a handgun. He advanced warily on Chance, who backed slowly away. As soon as he was close enough, Bannock swung the pistol in an arc. Chance ducked, throwing his arm up to try to deflect the blow. Even so, it caught him a nasty crack on the side of the head and Chance collapsed to his knees.

"No," the Tiger said calmly as Bannock stepped forward to strike again.

"You're finished, Quilch," Chance told the Tiger before

Bannock could object. "Scevola and his people are here. Harm them and some rather influential Italian families will hunt you down and rip out your guts. And that's just for starters."

"I told you," Bannock hissed. "We should get out now."

"I won't lose the money," the Tiger insisted. "We don't have time—"

"You have plenty of time," Chance told him. "I see you know about the diamond. But what you don't know is that the nine o'clock deadline was a bluff—a way of smoking out who the Tiger really is. And it worked. Run while you can. Hide, for a while. Spend the money quickly because if Scevola doesn't get you, Ardman will."

The Tiger shook with anger. He stuffed the diamond and the magnifying glass into his jacket pocket. "Bring them," he ordered. "All of them."

It was a shock for Jade to realize he was talking to her. She nodded, trying to look like she was a butch mercenary working for a rich madman, and pushed Rich ahead of her, gesturing for the Banker to follow.

The only other guards were Bannock and the technician. Bannock motioned for Chance to follow, while the technician quickly closed the laptop and pushed it into a soft leather case.

"There isn't room for all of us in the helicopter," Bannock said as they hurried down the corridor toward the castle courtyard.

"Then not all of us will be leaving," the Tiger told him. "Oh, don't worry—I need you, Bannock. You're the only one of us here who can fly the thing." He turned to the technician. "And I suppose I need you too. Which rather reduces the options."

"Then let us go," suggested Chance.

They emerged into the courtyard. The helicopter the Tiger had arrived in was standing to one side, a second helicopter from the raid on the school behind it. Across from them, several of Bannock's guards had taken cover and were trying to hold back Scevola's men. Slowly but surely, the men in dark suits were advancing into the castle.

Behind them, Jade could see Ralph and Halford looking remarkably relaxed as they sat with their backs to one of the stone walls, watching the firefight. Ralph was smoking a cigar.

"You don't need us—not even the Banker," Chance said. "Not now that you've got the diamond."

"I certainly don't need *you*," the Tiger said.

Bannock leveled his gun at Chance. But the Tiger waved him away.

"I have a better idea. Call it insurance. You think Ardman will come after me? Well, then it is up to you to persuade him that isn't such a good idea."

"And why would I do that?" Chance had to shout over the noise of the gunfire.

"Because I have your son as a hostage."

Bannock was grinning as he turned toward Rich. "Take him to the helicopter."

"No!" Chance shouted. "Wait! Take me instead. He's just a boy."

The Tiger smiled. "Give me your gun," he told Bannock. "Then get into the helicopter." He glanced at Jade. "Yes, you too—if there's room."

Bannock grabbed Rich and dragged him over to the helicopter. The technician ran ahead and pulled the side door open to allow Bannock to bundle Rich inside. Jade was close behind. She waited beside the open door.

The Tiger was covering Chance and the Banker with the gun. "So, this is goodbye. I do hope you manage to persuade Ardman that you should get the opportunity to see your son again." He backed away toward the helicopter.

"I'm so sorry," the Banker said.

"It's not over yet," Chance told him.

Jade waited for the Tiger to get to the helicopter. She wondered if she should salute but decided against it.

"It is a bit of a tight fit," he said as he reached the door. "I think perhaps you can stay and help keep our Italian friends busy."

"Sir," Jade said as gruffly as possible. What now? She did the only thing she could think of. She held her hand out to the Tiger as he prepared to climb into the helicopter and demanded, "Gun."

Without thinking and needing both hands to climb in, he handed Jade his gun.

And as soon as he was inside, she leaned into the helicopter and pointed it squarely at the Tiger. "Don't move."

The engines were powering into life. Bannock, at the

controls, didn't see and couldn't hear what was happening behind him.

"Rich!" Jade yelled above the engines. "Get over here—come on!"

The technician was covering Rich with a gun. Jade yelled at him too. "Put that down or I shoot the Tiger."

The technician quickly placed the gun on the floor. Rich scrambled across the helicopter. But just as he reached the door, the huge rotor blades began to swing. The noise and the draft distracted Jade for a second. Just long enough for the Tiger to grab for the gun. Jade held on. Rich tried to help, and the gun skidded across the floor out of everyone's reach. But the technician was picking up his gun again.

A shot hammered past Jade. Rich jumped. The Tiger lunged at him—caught him by the arm, dragging him back into the helicopter just as the huge craft began to lift from the flagstones.

Chance and the Banker ran toward the helicopter, battling against the wind from the rotors. The Banker was knocked over backward by the force of it, but Jade leaped and grabbed for Rich as he dangled from the doorway. The Tiger still had one of Rich's arms. Jade had the other one and the help of gravity. But could she get Rich free before she too was lifted off the ground?

The Tiger was losing his grip. He clawed at Rich's arm, elbow, wrist, trying desperately to hold on. But when Chance reached past Jade and managed to get hold of Rich's shoulder, the battle was won. They all fell as the helicopter rose into the sky. The three of them—father, son and daughter—landed in an untidy heap. Bruised, battered and laughing.

"I don't know why I'm laughing," Rich said as they picked themselves up. He rubbed at his sore wrist. "That maniac got my watch!"

The gunfire had stopped. With the departure of the Tiger, his few remaining guards had given up. Scevola was talking angrily to Ralph. He snapped his fingers and pointed to the castle gates. The men in suits were heading back to their boat.

All except Ralph. He called something after Scevola and then walked slowly over to where Chance, the Banker, Halford, Jade and Rich were standing.

"Not a problem, I hope?" Chance said.

Ralph shrugged. "Scevola tells me this is all my fault and when he reports to his colleagues, I will be held to account."

"You don't seem very worried."

"Not unduly."

"Won't they kill you?" Rich asked.

"Only if Scevola delivers his report. Otherwise, who is to say that it wasn't his fault and that I was lucky to escape with my life and my freedom?"

It was strangely quiet now that the shooting had stopped and the helicopter was gone. The only noise was the sound of the boat's engine. Rich could see through the main gateway that the boat was fading into the distance.

"And why might Scevola not deliver his report?" Halford asked.

The answer was the dull *thump* of an explosion. The distant boat had disappeared in a huge orange fireball. Black smoke billowed up into the sky.

"I gave him a present," Ralph said, without turning to look. "And speaking of presents," he said to Chance before anyone could comment, "I hope you will put in a good word for me with Mr. Ardman. I could have gotten Scevola his money, but it would have meant the loss of a fine watch."

"What do you mean?" Jade said.

"Don't ask me," Rich said. "I've lost mine already."

"Actually," Chance said, "I might put in a good word. If you *can* arrange for the loss of that watch."

Ralph frowned. "Why? Where is it?"

The helicopter's radar had detected several other aircraft heading for the island of Calder. Bannock had been right, the Tiger thought—better to get out while they could. Scevola's men had been enough trouble. The SAS would be another story altogether.

And all he had lost was time. He had the satellite connection and laptop; he had the diamond with the account numbers and access codes. And, he realized as it beeped in his hand, he had the Chance boy's rather expensive watch.

Yes—all in all, not a bad day's work. He reached out to pat Bannock appreciatively on the shoulder. Bannock turned slightly and smiled through his fierce red beard.

The watch was still beeping. It felt hot in the Tiger's hand. The beeping was getting louder and more insistent, and the

Tiger frowned. A rather nasty thought had just occurred to him.

"Open the door," he yelled at the technician.

But his words were lost in the sound of the explosion. Debris rained down on the sea far below—plastic, metal, dead bodies . . . And a large diamond that made barely a splash as it hit the water and sank forever into its depths.

The three olive green helicopters only just fit inside the castle next to the other helicopter. Maybe they were bored, Jade thought, but the SAS men had insisted on going through every room to check for the Tiger's guards. Every so often she could hear a shout of, "Clear!" or the *crump* of a grenade.

Ardman also seemed disappointed. And he seemed most disappointed to learn that Ralph had been responsible for the destruction of the Tiger's helicopter as the man fled.

"We couldn't have done it without him, sir," Chance said.

"I'll vouch for that," Halford agreed.

So, reluctantly, Ardman agreed to allow Ralph to leave and return to Krejikistan. "Just don't come back," he said.

Police launches were arriving at the dock, and Ralph said goodbye to them all before going to beg a lift back to the mainland. "The boat I came in also met with a slight accident," he explained straight-faced to Ardman.

"I can imagine," Ardman replied.

Ralph shook hands with Halford and Rich. He gave Jade

a kiss on the cheek and then enfolded Chance in a sudden bear hug.

"That necklace he gave you," Chance said as Ralph walked away.

"What about it?" Jade was still wearing it, she realized, under her guard's jacket.

"Nothing," her father said. "I might have to take off one of the glass beads, that's all."

"Well." Ardman sighed. "I suppose all's well that ends well. We won't be getting the money, but neither will the Tiger." He looked at the Banker, who was standing a little sheepishly in the background. "Don't worry—we'll still honor our side of the bargain."

"Thank you," the Banker said. "But I think Rich has something to tell you that may help."

Rich gasped. "I almost forgot."

"What?" Dad asked.

"Before the Tiger got the diamond, we used the lens from an old telescope and copied down the account numbers and the codes. I've got them here."

He pulled off one of his shoes and produced a folded sheet of lined notepaper.

Ardman took the paper and unfolded it. "Remarkable," he breathed. "This is just what we need." He folded the paper up again and put it in his pocket. Then he turned to the Banker. "I'm sorry, I was forgetting my manners. I have a nice surprise for you too."

The Banker looked confused and worried as Ardman turned

and waved to a soldier standing by one of the helicopters. "Yes, now, please!" he shouted.

The soldier nodded and opened the door of the helicopter. A figure stepped carefully out. She looked pale and needed the soldier's help to walk slowly and stiffly across the courtyard. Her distinctive long auburn hair fluttered in the breeze.

"Eleri?" the Banker gasped. He moved very fast for such a short man, running to her. The soldier stepped aside, letting father and daughter hug each other in the castle courtyard.

The others were distracted from watching the tearful reunion by the arrival of a uniformed policeman. "Anyone here named Chance?" he asked.

"Take your pick," Ardman said. "Which one do you want? We've got the whole family."

"I'm after the one who took a car from someone called Flip." The policeman held up a cell phone. "Apparently, they promised they'd look after it and return it in one piece. What shall I tell him?"

"Taking a car?" Rich asked.

"A promise is a promise," Jade told her father.

"I'm sure we can sort out any small problems," Ardman said. "I'm thinking of getting Sir Lionel's replacement to set up a special transport fund just for you, actually."

Chance smiled and turned to the policeman. "Well, technically it *is* in one piece. Or near enough anyway. There's no problem. Really. And you can tell him—I even gave it a wash."

Turn the page for a preview of

SHARP SHOT

Jack Higgins's next novel with Justin Richards

1

The present day. Gloucestershire, England.

Jade Chance was out jogging. The route she took—through the village and back across the hills—was almost exactly six and a half kilometers. She tried to run every day after school, and occasionally she persuaded her brother, Rich, to go with her. But not this afternoon.

When he was at home, Dad often joined her. Jade had expected him to be slow and out of shape; he ate the most appalling rubbish, he smoked—though less than he used to—and as far as Jade could tell, he drank only black coffee, beer and champagne. Sometimes together. But he always surprised her by keeping up.

It was November, so it was already dark when Jade got back. She'd left Rich doing his homework, and he was still at it when she returned.

"Dad phoned," said Rich, without looking up. He was sitting at the dining table in the main living room of the small cottage the three of them shared on the outskirts of the small village in the heart of the Cotswold hills.

"Did he say where he is or what he's doing?" Jade asked, going straight through to the kitchen.

"Nope."

"Did he say when he'll be back?" Jade called as she opened the fridge.

"In a few days"

"Did he say where he's put the can opener?"

"Nope," Rich called back. "But I did ask," he added after a moment.

"Liar." Jade started to unload the beer and champagne from the fridge. "So why did he bother to call?"

"Don't know. That was something I *didn't* ask." Rich was standing in the doorway, watching Jade empty the fridge. "I hope you're not going to empty all that down the sink again," he said.

"No. But I don't see why the fridge has to be full of Dad's booze. One bottle of champagne and two bottles of beer, that's what he's allowed now. If you've finished your homework, you can go online and order some real food and drink."

"You mean healthy stuff." Rich was smiling. "You mean lettuce and carrots and things that only rabbits eat. You mean fruit juice and bottled water."

"Among other things." Jade stood up and surveyed the collection of bottles on the countertop. "That should do it. If we're left on our own to look after ourselves, we might as well eat healthily and sensibly while we can. After all, if he's working for Ardman, he could be anywhere in the world for days or weeks or even months, I guess."

"Yeah," Rich agreed. "I did an order yesterday, anyway. They're supposed to deliver it this evening. Don't worry, I put us down for some health food. Salad and fruit and vegetables. Oh, and I ordered some Coke and burgers too. And we can have pizza tonight." He grinned at Jade's horrified expression. "You can put extra pineapple on yours. Then it'll count as fruit."

Before Jade could protest, her phone beeped. It was warning her it was almost out of power, so she went through to her bedroom to plug it into the charger. By the time she returned, Rich was back at his homework.

There was something else Jade was determined to do while Dad was away. That was to unpack at least some of the crates and boxes that had been standing unopened in the spare room since they'd arrived several months earlier.

Dad was used to living out of suitcases and boxes, but since the death of the twins' mother, Jade hadn't really felt anywhere was home. If she unpacked Dad's stuff, if they filled the cottage with things that belonged to them as a family rather than the people they were renting the cottage from, then maybe this would become home.

It frustrated Jade that Rich didn't seem to have the same problem. Maybe he was more like their dad. He seemed happy just to unpack things as and when—and if—he needed them. If she left it to the men, Jade knew, they'd never be moved in.

Another reason for unpacking, though she could barely admit it to herself, was that despite everything, Jade was enjoying her new life. Dad could be annoying and irritating, but he'd demonstrated time and again the lengths he'd go to for his children. It was strange to think that less than a year ago, John Chance hadn't even known he *had* children, and they'd known nothing about him . . .

School was okay, and Jade had made some friends. There was a time, a few months back, when she'd expected to be asked to leave. But Dad's boss, Ardman, had somehow persuaded the headmaster and board of governors that getting involved in an armed siege during which large sections of the school were blown up and other parts demolished by various members of the Chance family—including Dad, who'd driven his BMW right through the main reception area—wasn't actually an expellable offense.

Somewhere at the back of Jade's mind was the thought that if she got everything unpacked, it would be that much more difficult, that much more unlikely, they would have to move on. The cottage might not seem quite like home yet, but she hoped it soon would.

"Box time!" she called to Rich as she packed the beer and champagne into a cupboard.

"What, again?"

"One a day, remember? We agreed." She went back through to the living room.

"We didn't agree," Rich told her. "You decided. An agreement requires the consent of both parties."

Jade sighed. It wasn't worth an argument. "You sort out the shopping," she said. "I'll do the box after I've had a shower. Deal?"

"I suppose."

Jade grinned. Her twin brother drove her every bit as crazy as her dad did. But she couldn't imagine being without him. She went into the bathroom, thinking how lucky she really was to have Dad and Rich. How lucky she was that no one had tried to kill her for months now.

Rich watched as Jade dragged a large cardboard box in from the spare room. She sat cross-legged on the floor beside it. Her shoulder-length fair hair was still wet, and she'd pulled on a sweatshirt and sweatpants.

"Anything good?" Rich asked.

"Books, papers, magazines." Jade pulled out a handful of magazines and spread them on the carpet beside her. "I mean, why does he keep this stuff?"

"You can always put it away again."

She was leafing through the different magazines—*National Geographic*, *The Rifleman*, *The Economist*, *History Today*, *Jane's Intelligence Review* . . . The books were just as varied. There was a battered hardback copy of *Oliver Twist* stacked with a book about the Falklands War. Jade pulled out a paperback thriller published in the 1970s. The cover was a photograph of a woman dressed in combat uniform. Or rather, half dressed in it. Jade tossed it to one side.

"That looks good," said Rich, kneeling down beside her.

"No, it doesn't," she told him. "Leave it where it is. That's the rubbish pile."

"Dad might want to read it again."

"You think he got past the front cover the first time?" Jade threw another paperback after it. It landed facedown.

"What was that one?" Rich asked eagerly.

"You don't want to know."

"You mean *you* don't want me to know."

Jade had lifted out a different stack of books and magazines. There was an old newspaper on the top. The headline read, GOVERNMENT DENIES SAS INVOLVEMENT IN HOSTAGE RESCUE. Underneath it was another paper—a lurid tabloid from the same day. Its headline was: OUR BOYS GIVE 'EM HELL.

"Wonder why he's kept these?" said Rich.

"Like we can't guess."

"Shall I put them with the photos?"

Jade nodded. "Good idea."

There was a small desk in the corner of the room, by the French doors. These opened onto a small patio overlooking the back garden. The desk had a sloping front that folded down to become a writing area. Behind it was a rack of pigeon-holes and compartments. Jade had found a stack of old photos in one of Dad's boxes and put them inside the desk. Since then, they had found several more to add to the collection.

The newspapers were too big to go with the photos, so Rich put them in an empty drawer in the bottom part of the desk. Jade seemed busy unpacking the box, so Rich opened the lid of the desk and took out the bundle of photographs.

There were maybe twenty or so, taken at different times in different places. Most of them showed John Chance—in army dress uniform, in a dinner suit, on an assault course covered in mud but grinning. There was a crumpled picture of Rich and Jade's mother. It was a small, creased, passport-sized shot, and it looked like it had been kept in a wallet or a pocket for years.

But the picture that intrigued Rich was a faded snapshot taken in the desert. At least, it looked like the desert—there was lots of sand, but the four men in it were standing in front of a low wall. All four were dressed in khaki army uniforms. One of them was a younger John Chance, another Rich and Jade knew was Dex Halford, who'd been in the SAS with their dad. They both looked so young—in their mid-twenties, Rich guessed.

One of the other two men was slightly shorter and stocky with a thin, dark mustache. He was standing beside John Chance, looking slightly wary. The fourth man was wiry and had a shock of hair the same color as the sand. He was grinning and pointing at the camera with one hand, while his other hand was resting on Dex Halford's shoulder.

On the back of the photo was written in ballpoint pen: *Iraq—November 1990. JC, DH, Mark and Ferdy.*

"What's that noise?" Jade asked suddenly.

Rich pushed the photos back inside the desk, dropped the newspapers in front of them and closed the lid. "I didn't hear anything."

"Sounded like thunder."

Rich pulled out his cell phone. "I'll check the forecast." He started up the Web browser. It drained the battery, but he enjoyed using it.

"Gadget man," said Jade. "Why don't you just look outside?"

"It's dark," Rich protested as he waited for the Web page to load.

"You can still tell if it's raining. Rain—you know, that wet stuff that drops from the sky."

"Nothing forecast," Rich told her.

He pushed his phone back into his pocket and opened the French doors. The evening was quite warm for late autumn. There was a half-moon, and the sky looked clear. Rich stepped out onto the patio. The security light on the wall above came on at once, detecting Rich's movement as he walked.

The small garden ended with a wooden fence made of thin panels. There was a gate that led out to the small wooded area beyond. Behind that were fields and a stream snaking through the hills. To Rich, brought up in an American city before the twins' mother brought them home to Britain, it seemed very isolated and quiet.

Now the quiet was shattered by the sound Jade had mistaken for thunder. Standing outside, Rich could hear it much more clearly. It was coming from the woods behind the house.

It was gunfire.

Rich stepped quickly back inside and locked the French doors.

Outside, the security light went off. The doors were reflective panels of black. Rich found himself looking at his own reflection, Jade standing beside him.

"Fireworks, do you think?" said Jade.

"No. Guns."

Typical, thought Jade. *Just when it seemed like we could finally settle down . . .*

"Might just be hunters," she said hopefully.

"At night?"

Jade sighed. "Okay, we'd better take cover. And call the police."

At that moment the security light came on again, bathing the patio in harsh white light.

Rich and Jade took a step backward as a dark shape approached the cottage. It crashed into the doors, bursting them open. A man staggered into the room, his eyes wide and staring. His face was caked in blood and his clothes were tattered and dirty.

Rich stared openmouthed. He knew the man. He'd been looking at his picture just now. He might be twenty years older, his sandy hair going gray, but it was obviously one of the men from the photograph taken in Iraq.

"Chance!" the man gasped. "Looking for John Chance. He's the only person who can help me now." The man collapsed to his knees, then toppled forward to fall motionless at Rich's feet.